"You mus[...] the local [...]

Nicola frow[...] "There are a n[...] working on the site," [...]nt on. "Their encampment is beyond our camp. But their women are protected more than ours. Your being here might cause a furor when the Sheikh finds out."

Nicola smiled. "The Sheikh!" she echoed softly. "How romantic."

Jason stared at her angrily. "For heaven's sake, don't get any ideas in that direction. They are men like other men, and they consider European women self-seeking and virtueless."

Nicola's eyes widened. "I can take care myself, Mr. Wilde. Not to worry."

"I don't," muttered Jason. "My only concern is the pipeline, not your person."

Nicola had never met such an infuriating man!

**ANNE MATHER**
is also the author of these books in

*Harlequin Presents Collection*

Many of these titles are available at your local bookseller.

# ANNE MATHER

## dark enemy

Originally published as Harlequin Presents # 26

## *Harlequin Books*

TORONTO • LONDON • LOS ANGELES • AMSTERDAM
SYDNEY • HAMBURG • PARIS • STOCKHOLM • ATHENS • TOKYO

Harlequin presents edition published November 1973
ISBN 0-373-15021-0

Second printing July 1974
Third printing August 1974
Fourth printing May 1976
Fifth printing September 1976
Sixth printing February 1977
Seventh printing March 1977

This *Harlequin Presents Collection* edition published July 1981

Original hardcover edition published in 1972
by Mills & Boon Limited

# CHAPTER ONE

It was hot, uncomfortably so, and inside the cloistered dwelling with its thick hanging tapestries and richly carved ceilings there was little air. A huge lamp made of bronze and burnished to a rich tone burned what little oxygen penetrated the thick walls, and not even the glowing arches, picked out with lapis lazuli, or the gold and blue mosaic of the floor could compensate for the cloying atmosphere of heavy perfume, strong wines, and the inherent scent of perspiring bodies.

The Sheikh Abi Ben Abdul Mohammed, lounging on cushions of satin and silk idly helping himself to handfuls of grapes, was every inch the eastern potentate and seemed totally oblivious of the heat or the unhealthy atmosphere. But Jason Wilde was aware of it, just as he was aware that the effort to control his temper was causing rivulets of sweat to slide down his spine, plastering his shirt to his back.

'Look, Mohammed,' he said tautly, 'we've got to get this settled. You know that and I know that, so we might as well come to an agreement.'

Sheikh Mohammed studied his companion rather appraisingly, and then said coolly: 'You must make the agreement, Wilde. After all, it is in your interests much more than mine!' His tones were smooth and slightly derogatory, and Jason felt an immense urge to lift him out of his bed of cushions and thrust his fist down his throat. It would be so easy and so enjoyable. The man was like a snake, deliberately causing unrest, arousing the men so that they didn't know where to turn, uncertain of their loyalties.

But he couldn't touch him. They were not individuals, and no amount of wishful thinking would alter the fact that he was the representative of Inter-Anglia Oil, just as the Sheikh was the ruler, and therefore the spokesman, of this small state of Abrahm.

So instead of reacting violently he said, equally coolly: 'Neverthless, Mohammed, it would be ludicrous of me to attempt to make any kind of agreement when I don't know exactly what it is you want.'

The Sheikh leaned forward and with slow and purposely languid movements helped himself to a cigarette, and after one of the attendants who stood rigidly to attention behind him had dashed forward to light his cigarette he drew on it deeply before speaking again.

Jason got to his feet. Sitting on the floor was not conducive to comfort when one's legs were long, and besides, the inactivity was infuriating. The Sheikh looked up at him rather derisively, and said:

'But, Wilde, you know what I want. I want my men to have a – square deal, just as your own men do. I do not feel that at present this is so. Besides, you are visitors here, never forget that, and as such are only welcome so long as your presence is not annoying to me.'

Jason thrust his hands into the pockets of the cotton pants he was wearing, and controlled his features. 'Without the resources of my company, Abrahm would not be able to mount such an operation,' he replied, quite expressionlessly.

The Sheikh shrugged. 'No. I agree, this is so. Nevertheless, without Abrahm's natural resources there would be no operation.'

Jason heaved a sigh. As always in matters of this kind, the Sheikh was overwhelmingly obtuse, constantly creating *impasse* in their discussions by remarks of this kind. There was no answer to him, and Jason knew that no matter how impatient he might become he would just have to wait until the Sheikh was prepared to state his demands without preamble.

But it was difficult to remain impassive when to add to the overheated atmosphere of the Sheikh's magnificent habitation there was Jason's own impatience at this needless delay. They met enough obstacles in the course of their work without meeting the unnecessary obstinacy of the Sheikh.

But now the Sheikh seemed to decide a change of subject was warranted, and with annoying urbanity, he said: 'Tell me, Wilde, what does a man like you derive from working here? You do not strike me as the kind of man who eschews the fleshpots for more, shall we say, aesthetic pursuits.'

Jason controlled his anger. It was typical that Mohammed should endeavour to direct the course of the conversation into these channels. He had an unhealthy interest in dissecting the men who came within his sphere, examining their lives and their motivations minutely.

'Abrahm is not the first Middle Eastern country I have worked in,' Jason said now. 'As a member of an oil company, one has to be prepared to work in any part of the world.'

'Yes?' The Sheikh sounded thoughtful. 'I suppose this is so. Nevertheless, I understand from reliable sources that you were offered a less active part in the proceedings, which you turned down.'

Jason wondered where the man obtained his information. His refusal to accept the board's generous offer of a seat at their table had shocked his contemporaries. But just at present it suited him to be out of England, and Sir Harold had made it plain the offer was still open.

'Your sources of information are very astute,' he remarked now, walking lazily across the room, as though uncaring of the swift passing of time. He picked up a small bronze statue and examined it in detail, while the Sheikh watched his movements and pondered the mind of this annoying foreigner who seemed totally indifferent to his own status here.

'So,' said the Sheikh at last, summoning one of his servants who produced a heavy ashtray for him to stub out his cigarette. 'We return to the subject in hand. You think perhaps I am being unkind when I say my people are being exploited?'

Jason swung round, a ready retort dying on his lips as he realized he had almost fallen again into the Sheikh's trap.

'Go on,' he said quietly.

'Very well. Would a few more pence bankrupt your company? I think not. The English and American oil barons are growing rich on the poverty of their investment areas. My people do not have television sets, or cars or even proper homes. The standard of living here in Abrahm is very low.'

Jason could have said that it would have been useless people having television sets in a country where there was no television station. He could have said that there was no money to build roads to drive cars along until the oil began pumping along the pipeline which was barely a third completed. He could have said that the oil company was providing work for those people to enable them to have a better standard of living.

But he said none of this. Instead, he allowed Mohammed to state his case, knowing full well that to argue would cause a stream of abuse, and possibly more trouble for the company in the long run. Eventually Mohammed grew tired of the Englishman's silence, and said: 'Well, Wilde! What is your answer? Are you prepared to listen to reason?'

'I'm prepared to listen to anything that is reasonable,' replied Jason dryly. 'All right, Mohammed, I've been in touch with London, and they have given me permission to offer you a two and a half pence increase.'

Sheikh Mohammed's lip curled. 'Five,' he said sharply.

Jason shrugged. 'Three – and that's my final offer.'

Sheikh Mohammed rubbed the side of his nose with a hand that literally glittered with the rings of emerald and ruby that sparkled there. Then he summoned one of his underlings and signified that he wished someone brought to the conference chamber. Jason moved restlessly, beginning to feel impatient again. Good God, how long was this going to go on? He glanced at the gold watch on his wrist, and gave an exclamation. It was already late afternoon and by the time he got back to the site the evening meal would be in the course of being prepared. That meant yet another day had been wasted.

Even so, it was pleasant to recall the comparative luxury of his air-conditioned bungalow, and the thought of a decent drink and some food was quite appealing. After all, it wasn't his fault they were being held up, although he seemed to bear the brunt of the complaints from the boardroom in London.

Sheikh Mohammed had summoned Krashki, his chief minister, and Jason was forced to kick his heels for almost another half hour while they talked in undertones, their gesticulations eloquent of their conversation. Eventually, when Jason was on the verge of walking out of the conference altogether, Mohammed turned to him, his expression brooding but subdued.

'Very well,' he said, getting to his feet, his flowing robes giving him a dignity that European clothes would not, 'we accept your terms. But it is to be understood that when Sir Harold Mannering comes out from England I shall discuss this further with him.'

He raised his hand as Jason would have replied, and swept out of the room like some emperor of old. His servants followed him closely and for a moment Jason remained where he was looking towards the doorway through which Sheikh Abi Ben Abdul Mohammed had passed. Then with an infuriated shake of his head he stood on the butt of his cigarette and strode after him, turning away from the inner quarters of the palace with its Moorish-styled architecture towards the searing blaze of the sunlit courtyard.

The brilliance of the sun was dazzling, and he slid his dark glasses on to his nose before walking swiftly across to where his Land-Rover was parked. He slid behind the wheel and heaved a sigh. There was a sense of relaxation in actual action after the enforced inactivity of the last couple of hours. Breathing deeply, he realized that anything was preferable to the cloying heat of the Sheikh's apartments.

Turning on the engine, he drove out of the courtyard, ignoring the stares of the guards on the gate, and quickly rolled up his windows as the vehicle encountered the track outside which was little more than an extension of that desert that stretched between here and the drilling site. He thought Abrahm was one of the most barren places on the earth. Situated between Tunisia and Libya, with a port on the Mediterranean, it had little to commend it.

He had several miles to cover between Abyrra and Castanya where the oil company had set up their camp of bungalows, and as he drove he wondered why he had not chosen a more amenable spot in which to work. In his position he could have chosen any one of a dozen locations, but he liked the crew at Castanya, and if there was little more in Abrahm than sand, sand and more sand he wasn't particularly bothered. He was not a man who desired a hectic social life and if the site got too boring for him there was always Gitana on the Mediterranean coast where a man could find entertainment in plenty.

He drove fast, his mind on the job ahead. Already they had wasted four days. Sheikh Mohammed was not the most reasonable of men. He used his influence carelessly, and had refused to meet anyone from the oil company until it suited his purpose. Even now, Jason was aware that the peace he had won was a precarious one and would only last as long as Sheikh Mohammed desired it to do so. There had been rumours of an uprising among the nomadic Bedouin tribes against the despotism of Mohammed, but Jason doubted whether anything would come of it. Either way the oil company stood in exactly the same position. They were a non-political enterprise and he doubted whether if Mohammed was overthrown their position would be any easier. Oil was the country's salvation; only the profits and the methods of its production could be in jeopardy.

The sun was beginning to go down when he mounted the high pass above the oil fields. In a country where inland there was so little vegetation, it was surprisingly beautiful, and only the stark drilling rigs gave any indication of the century they were living in. The desert was unchanging in its isolation, and the rocks threw back the rays of the setting sun in colours of red and orange and purple. The distant mountain range was tinged with the palest of mauves while the stars were beginning to glimmer in the velvet of the night sky. He descended the pass, crossed the stretch of desert between the rocks and the camp, and entered the small community of bungalows. The oil company had provided every amenity for its men, even to the extent of mounting a swimming pool, the water of which was rarely cool but always refreshing. There was a canteen, but some of the men preferred to cater for themselves. Jason was one of these, and as he also had rather a good cook-boy in the person of Ali, he managed very well. He had known Ali for several years, first meeting him when he was working on the Gulf. Since then, Ali had visited a great number of places with him, but he always liked to return to his desert birthplace.

As he reached the office building where the paperwork of the site and its accompanying pipeline was maintained, his second-in-command, Graham Wilson, came dashing out to meet him, waving his arms about vigorously, obviously desiring Jason to stop.

Jason brought the Land-Rover to a halt, and wound down the window, reaching for his cigarettes in the breast pocket of his cream denim shirt.

'Yeah!' he said resignedly. 'What now?'

Wilson wrenched open the door of the Land-Rover and slid inside. Glancing round rather surreptitiously, he said: 'How are things with you?'

Jason frowned. 'Could be worse. Why?'

Graham Wilson hunched his shoulders. 'Get an eyeful of that, over there!' He pointed towards a low-slung black limousine, now sadly covered in fine dust but still magnificently designed.

Jason looked, put a cigarette between his lips, and as he flicked his lighter, said: 'Who's arrived?' rather laconically. He didn't feel he had the strength to instil himself with any more annoyance today, not after the last couple of hours with Sheikh Mohammed.

'Mannering!' said Graham dramatically.

'*Mannering!*' echoed Jason, taking the cigarette out of his mouth. 'What in hell does Mannering want? I thought he left it to me to deal with this!'

'Not Mannering, senior,' exclaimed Graham, with the air of one who is imparting a confidence. '*Paul* Mannering! And he's not alone, either. He's brought his – er – secretary with him!'

'God Almighty!' Jason stared at Graham disbelievingly. 'That little punk out here! What in hell for?'

Graham half-smiled. 'I thought you'd be pleased, Jason. Wait till you get a load of the secretary, though!'

'I'll get a load of nobody!' snapped Jason violently. 'For heaven's sake, Graham, is old Mannering going out of his mind? Sending that pip-squeak out here! But why? Why?'

Graham shrugged. 'Well, as I hear it, old Mannering's cut up rough about the way Paul's been living. You know what I mean. Anyway, there was a cable came, just after you left for Abyrra, announcing that he was sending Paul out here to learn the oil business from the bottom up. He said he'd be getting in touch with you to give you a fuller picture.'

'Decent of him!' muttered Jason savagely. 'But where does this secretary come in? I mean – does *Daddy* know about her?'

'Your guess is as good as mine,' replied Graham, shrugging. 'Quite honestly, I can't believe he does. But I'm not grumbling. It's so long since I've seen a white woman—'

'Pack it in, Graham,' said Jason bleakly. 'It's exactly three months since you saw a white woman. Besides, remember you've a wife back in England!'

'Just because I've bought a book doesn't mean I can't join the library,' retorted Graham, with a grin. And then: 'Anyway, it's not my problem. It's yours.'

Jason nodded. 'Where are they?'

'In there.' Graham jerked his head back towards the office building. 'I didn't know what else to do with them until you returned. Coming to meet them?'

Jason shrugged and then slid wearily out of the vehicle. 'Do I have any choice?' he questioned dryly. 'Okay, okay, let's go. But I could surely use a shower and a change of clothes.'

Graham led the way up wooden steps into the air-conditioned office building. They entered a long narrow hallway with several doors opening from it. Graham opened the first of these and they entered a room of generous proportions entirely dominated by the heavy desk that stood square in the centre of the polished wooden floor. Perched on a corner of the desk was a young woman smoking a cigarette and passing the time by blowing smoke-rings into the air. At the far side of the desk a young man was standing staring through the meshed grill of the window, but he turned abruptly at their entrance and gave Jason a derogatory glance. 'Well, well,' he remarked, rather sarcastically,

'Wilde himself! Surprise, surprise!'

The girl had slid off the desk now and also stood regarding him, a strange expression in the depths of eyes that were amazingly green. They were set in a face that while not possessing actual beauty held character and animation, and Jason understood why Graham had been so enthusiastic. Honey-gold hair hung to her shoulders, and was at present controlled by a wide band round her head. She was wearing mud-coloured levis and a cream shirt, and the masculine attire accentuated rather than detracted from her femininity.

'Well,' said Paul Mannering again. 'Aren't you going to say anything, Jason? I gather from Wilson that you didn't know we were coming.'

'No, I did not,' agreed Jason, folding his arms and regarding them coolly, his cigarette between his lips. 'Perhaps you'd better tell me first of all why this young woman is here. You – we can leave till later!' There was insolence in his tone.

Paul Mannering's face flushed with colour, but the girl didn't turn a hair. She merely took a final draw on her own cigarette, blew a couple more smoke-rings, and then stood on the stub, almost defiantly. Jason felt angry. How dared Harold Mannering send his son out here without warning, with or without announcement? Who the hell did he think he was? Why should he, Jason, have to make a man out of a layabout like Paul Mannering? And what was more to the point of the infuriation he was feeling, how dared Paul Mannering bring his current girl-friend with him, just for kicks? Surely he knew his father wouldn't stand for that!

'This young woman is Nicola King,' said Paul now, his colour subsiding a little, and a belligerent expression taking its place. 'Contrary to the lurid ideas that are buzzing round your brain she is not my responsibility. She's all Dad's.'

Jason's brows drew together in a dark scowl. 'What does that mean?'

The girl moved, and a half-smile lifted the corners of her mouth. 'It means, Mr. Wilde, that I am what I told your Mr. Wilson I am, a secretary, nothing more, nothing less.'

Jason gave her a scathing look. 'And what are you doing here, Miss King? Inter-Anglia needs no secretaries in the middle of the Abyrra desert. Or has Mannering taken leave of his senses? After all, sending Paul out here is hardly the action of a sensible man!'

'You watch your tongue,' snapped Paul Mannering angrily.

'I'm not a contortionist,' muttered Jason, taking his cigarette out of his mouth. 'Miss King, suppose you explain a little more!'

Nicola King stretched, drawing attention to the curving slenderness of her body. 'Mr. Wilde, we have been travelling since early this morning. I am hot and tired, and as we have been hanging around here for the best part of two hours waiting for you to return I don't think it's unreasonable to request that we be allowed a shower, a change of clothes and something to eat before feeling inclined to answer your rather obvious questions. Believe me, my reasons for being here are strictly non-social. If I had wanted an exciting life, I would hardly have chosen an oil drilling rig, miles out in the desert, where the heat and the flies and the total absence of civilized pursuits make my toes curl!'

Jason's eyes narrowed. He couldn't help but admire her spirit. She had more confidence than Mannering's son, even if he had had a public school education and delighted in making the headlines with one or other of his crazy schemes. But that did not endear her to Jason. He considered her self-opinionated and hard, and he speculated cynically on her relationship to the Mannerings. If she was not Paul's girl-friend, he deplored the methods she must have used to get Harold Mannering to allow her to come out here.

'Graham,' he said harshly, 'take the *lady* to Caxton's bungalow. See she has everything she wants, and after she's improved her temper as well as her appearance, bring her over to my place.'

Graham nodded, and Nicola King was forced to accompany him out of the door. But the glance she cast in Jason's direction was killing. Already the swift African night was falling and outside a velvety darkness melted the heat of the day. After they had gone, Jason leaned back against the door and studied his chairman's son rather disparagingly.

'Now,' he said, 'what's the idea?'

Mannering's eyes widened. 'Idea? What idea? Do you mean me being here? Or Nicola?'

'A little of both.'

'Like I said, it's nothing to do with me. Do you imagine I asked to come out here? Good God, if there'd been any way of getting out of it I would have taken it.

18

But while my hands are tied, moneywise—' He shrugged his slim shoulders. 'Anyway, it can't last.'

'What can't?'

'Me, being out here!' Paul fumbled for his cigarettes and then muttered: 'Thanks' as Jason offered him one. When it was lit he continued: 'I suppose you'll get all the sordid details from Dad so I might as well tell you my story first. There was this girl—'

'There always is,' remarked Jason laconically.

'Yeah, I know. And I'm always the sucker! But this doll was crazy about me, and I'm only human after all. How was I to know she'd take me seriously? Anyway, it turned out her dad was an ex-wrestler or something. He practically kidnapped me one night after I'd stopped seeing her. He went berserk!' Paul's young face blanched at the memory. 'Anyhow, to cut a long story short, the police were called and the press got to know and there was a God-awful stink! You can imagine what kind of coverage it got. The girl said she was pregnant, but she wasn't, our doctor proved that, thank heaven! But naturally it's left a pretty nasty situation, and Dad thought it was time I got out of the country for a while. I agreed. I didn't know he had this in mind.'

Jason's dark brows were raised. 'I see,' he said thoughtfully. 'I guessed as much. How old are you now, Paul – twenty, twenty-one? Hell, I don't ever remember being as young as you!'

'I'm twenty-two, actually,' replied Paul sullenly. 'You're not so different. What about that Ellis woman?'

Jason shrugged. 'A little different, I think, Paul. Anyway, that's beside the point, I suppose. You're here now, and we're stuck with you. But by heaven, you're not going to lie around here. You'll work, boy, believe me, you'll work!'

Paul's colour deepened again. 'Dad knew what he was doing when he sent me here, didn't he?' he muttered. 'Home from bloody home!'

'Never mind, kid. He may take pity on you. But that still doesn't explain that girl's arrival. Who the hell is she? If she's not your girl-friend, what is she?'

'You'd better wait and ask Dad,' retorted Paul, sniffing. 'Now, where do I shack down?'

Jason straightened, and opened the door, pausing momentarily in the aperture. 'I guess you could share with young Collins,' he said. 'He's one of the drilling crew. He's about your age.'

'I'd prefer to be alone,' said Paul moodily.

'I expect you would. However, there are only a certain number of bungalows here, and Caxton's is only empty because he's home on compassionate leave. His wife's just had their fifth child. So for the present, you'll have to be content with sharing with Collins. That is, unless you can persuade your travelling companion that her journey wasn't really necessary?'

'I've told you,' exclaimed Paul. 'Nicola is not my concern.'

Jason studied him a moment, and then shrugged. 'Okay, let's go. I'll drop you off and introduce you to Collins on my way to my bungalow. He'll take you over to the cookhouse later, and see you get a meal.

Tomorrow we'll consider what we can find for you to do.'

After he had got Paul settled with young Tony Collins, Jason drove thankfully to his own bungalow, and after parking the Land-Rover, mounted the steps wearily. Ali met him in the hall.

'At last you have come,' he said complainingly. 'The meal – it has been ready this half-hour.'

Jason grimaced. 'Well, I guess it'll have to wait another half-hour, Ali. I'm hot and sweaty, and I need a shower, not to mention a change of clothes.'

Ali pulled a long-suffering face, but Jason merely gave him a pat on the back and walked into his bedroom. The shower, despite being lukewarm, was refreshing, and clean cotton pants and a thin cotton knitted shirt felt good. He combed his thick hair, and re-entered the hall to cross it to the lounge. The bungalows were simply constructed with one long room serving as dining room and lounge, and the other side of the central hall was divided into bedroom and bathroom. The oil company erected these air-conditioned living quarters wherever they went, providing civilized accommodation for men who spent hours daily in entirely uncivilized conditions. Ali's quarters and the kitchen were out back, while at the front of the building was a verandah where one could sit in the cool of the evening. And the evenings could be very cold.

But now Jason was glad to accept the iced lager that Ali had waiting for him in the lounge and stifled an angry exclamation when the telephone rang insistently. Lifting the receiver, he said: 'Wilde speaking,' in a curt

21

tone.

'Jason? Is that you?' The voice was faint but familiar.

'Yes, Harold, it's me,' said Jason dryly, recognizing the voice of his superior back in London.

'You sound angry, Jason,' said Sir Harold Mannering, chuckling. 'I gather Paul and Nicola have arrived. Am I right?'

Jason swallowed half his lager at a gulp. 'You're damn right,' he answered, wiping his mouth with the back of his hand. 'What's the idea? Unloading your problems on to me?'

'Oh, you can handle Paul, Jason. Has he told you what happened here?'

'His version,' remarked Jason coldly. 'Okay, I admit, Paul doesn't cause many problems, but why send the girl?'

Sir Harold laughed. 'Now you must confess, it wasn't such an unpleasant surprise, was it?' he said cheerfully.

Jason's brows drew together frowningly. 'Have you taken leave of your senses, Harold?' he muttered. 'Sending a girl like that out here when I already have problems enough with the men!'

Sir Harold sounded less amiable. 'Steady on, Jason,' he said shortly. 'You aren't chairman yet, you know.'

Jason breathed hard through his nose. 'Harold,' he said tightly, 'I want Nicola King back in England at the earliest opportunity.'

Sir Harold cleared his throat. 'Are you ordering me, Jason?'

Jason sighed. 'Hell, no, Harold! Look, try to see it my way, if Paul needs a feminine shoulder to cry on, let him take himself off to Gitana like the rest of the crew. Why should he bring his girl-friend out here? I warn you – the men won't like it.'

Sir Harold's amiability returned. 'Now I know you're joking, Jason,' he said, chuckling. 'You know damn nicely, Nicola's not interested in Paul.'

Jason ran a hand across his forehead. He was tired and in need of sleep, and Sir Harold's words were not making sense any more. Making a last attempt to understand the situation, he said:

'Okay, okay, Harold. Why is she here?'

Sir Harold seemed to hesitate. 'Well, she's a pretty good secretary, Jason. She's worked in my office for the last eleven months, and I'm pretty sure you need some help with those reports. Don't deny that they're always late in arriving. Look here, the girl wanted to come out with Paul, and while I know it's irregular, well – I'm sure you can handle it.'

Jason shook his head, finished his lager and signalled to Ali to provide him with another. 'How long am I expected to keep her here?' he said tautly. 'I warn you – this is your responsibility, not mine.'

Sir Harold sniffed. 'Well, I must admit, you're a pretty ungrateful devil, Jason,' he said broodingly. 'Anyway, Nicola has another assignment. She's to keep an eye on Paul for me. I don't trust that boy out of my sight.'

'Short of running amok in a harem, there's little trouble he can get himself into here,' returned Jason sarcastically. 'Anyway, to introduce more mundane problems, I'm happy to state that the men return to work tomorrow.'

'Ah, you've seen Mohammed, then?'

'Yes, this afternoon.'

'What percentage?'

'Three.'

'Good, good!' Sir Harold sounded delighted. 'You've done well Jason. I'm immensely pleased. I'm sure the board will be, too.'

Jason grimaced. 'Don't I warrant a bonus?' he asked dryly.

'You surely do.'

'Then take the girl back!' Jason's tones were flat.

'Give her a chance, Jason,' exclaimed Sir Harold. 'Heck, she's just arrived. Let her prove herself. Don't be so stubborn!'

'Prove herself?' Jason shook his head again. 'You're losing me again, Harold. Okay, okay, leave it for now. I'll handle it. I'm too tired right now to argue with you.'

Sir Harold hung up chuckling, and after he had replaced his receiver Jason sat staring at the phone with puzzled eyes. It wasn't like Sir Harold to be so obtuse. What in hell did he think he was doing? Unless he imagined that by sending a suitable applicant out to Castanya he might persuade him to give up his bachelor status. For long enough Sir Harold had been trying to get him settled. Maybe this was his final effort. Even so, it was an unsatisfactory solution, but the only one he could come up with.

## CHAPTER TWO

In the absent Caxton's bungalow, Nicola King was taking a shower. The water which sprayed from the tank was warm, but invigorating, and she moved beneath its spray sensuously, loving the feel of the water against her hot skin. Despite the primitive conditions she was experiencing a sense of well-being and satisfaction. She was here, at Castanya; and there was absolutely nothing Jason Wilde could do about it.

She smiled as she recalled his outraged anger when he had discovered her presence on the site. Perhaps he had had enough of women for the time being, but she intended to see that he changed his mind. And then ...

Her expression hardened. Jason Wilde would find out that there were still some things he had to learn. He was so big, so powerful, so arrogantly assured of himself. Well, she would change all that. Just how, she was not sure. But she would find a way, of that she was certain. After all, everything had gone according to plan so far. She was here, when everything had been against her achieving such a thing. She gave a slight grimace. It hadn't been easy. Sir Harold had had to be persuaded, cajoled, gently flattered. He was a man like other men. And Nicola knew she was a woman men found attractive. Besides, there had been a sense of power in controlling a man like Sir Harold

Mannering.

She turned off the shower, and stepped out of the cubicle. Wrapping herself in the voluminous folds of a huge bathsheet, she wound it sarong-wise round her body and walked into the bedroom. Seating herself on the bed, she began to brush her thick hair until it was a sleek corn-coloured curtain about her shoulders. As she studied her appearance in the mirror of the dressing table she felt a faint twinge of regret, of conscience, almost. Was that hard-eyed creature intent on revenge really herself? Was *she* really determining to wreck a man's life? Where was her warmth and gentleness? Where was the eager young woman with confidence in herself and a zest for life?

She looked away from her image. That girl was gone – for ever. Banished by the careless actions of the man she had met only half an hour ago. Not that he was aware of the havoc he had wrought in her life. She doubted very much whether he was aware of the full extent of the havoc he had wrought in her sister's life. But he would become aware of it, of that she had no doubt. And when he did – then she would have her revenge.

She dressed in a slim-fitting shift of apricot cotton, left her hair loose about her shoulders, and applied a little eye-shadow and some lipstick. It was no good endeavouring a full make-up. The heat would cake foundation applications to her skin in no time.

As she was completing her toilet she heard a tapping at the door of the bungalow, and she emerged into the hall, and called 'Come in!'

Graham Wilson came through the door, smiling broadly. 'Well?' he said cheerfully. 'Did you find everything you needed?'

Nicola smiled back. 'Yes,' she said, nodding. 'Thank you.' She glanced into the lounge. 'Won't you come in? I think there are some drinks in the cabinet there.'

Graham flushed. 'Er – no, thanks, if you don't mind. Jason is expecting you, and I think we ought to be going.'

Nicola nodded understandingly. 'Ah, I see. Mr. Wilde. You find him a hard taskmaster?'

'Heck, no!' Graham was youthfully vehement. 'Jason's a grand chap to work with. All the fellows like him. But he hasn't much patience with late-comers, and he knows I came to collect you.'

Nicola decided this was no time to attempt to alienate the image Graham Wilson had of his boss, so she just said: 'Hang on while I get my bag,' and then followed him out of the bungalow.

They walked to Jason Wilde's bungalow, and it gave Nicola a chance to take a more detailed look at the site. The rows of living quarters edged a central highway, and at the far end a long low building was brightly lit, the music emanating from its interior indicating that this must be some sort of social centre.

Graham, sensing her speculation, said: 'That's the clubhouse. There's a pool out back of there, and we really appreciate it after a day at the rig. Most of the men work a shift system, and the clubhouse is open day and night. There's a restaurant,' – he grinned, 'I guess you'd call it a canteen, and the men can get a meal when they finish their stint. They work four days on and three off, generally. There are no accepted weekends here, like back home, and every month the men get a full week's leave. Usually they go down to Gitana, on the coast. There's plenty of activity at Gitana.'

'So I noticed,' remarked Nicola, nodding. 'Our plane came down there. We drove through the town. It's a little like Port of Spain, isn't it?'

'You've been to Trinidad?' Graham sounded surprised.

'Just a couple of months ago. With Sir Harold.'

'Oh, I see. I didn't realize—' Graham broke off his train of thought. 'Tell me, Miss King, how did you persuade our chairman to allow you to come out here?'

Nicola smiled. 'That's my secret,' she replied evenly. 'How about you? How long do you expect to be out here?'

'Until the pipeline's working. Right now it's barely a third completed. That's Jason's problem. The local Sheikh is making things pretty difficult for us.'

Nicola nodded. 'I see. What do you think Paul will have to do?'

'Mannering?' Graham shrugged. 'I don't know. Probably Jason will fix him up. Does he like getting his hands dirty?'

'I really couldn't say.' Nicola was brief, and then they had reached the bungalow where Jason was living.

'Here we are,' called Graham, mounting the steps ahead of Nicola, and leading the way into the lounge.

Jason Wilde was lounging in a chair, a glass of lager in his fingers, and he glanced up wryly at their entrance. 'You're a little late for dinner, Miss King,' he remarked sardonically.

Nicola, who was feeling ravenously hungry now, felt furiously angry. She was sure he was well aware of her emptiness, and had deliberately eaten early to force her into waiting until their interview was over when she would have to go to the eating place where all the men would be gathered.

However, she was an adept at concealing her feelings, and she replied, quite coolly: 'That's perfectly all right, Mr. Wilde. I can wait until later. Perhaps Mr. Wilson would be so kind as to bring a tray to my bungalow?'

Graham was about to accept this proposition when Jason got broodingly to his feet. 'My men are not waiters,' he said harshly. 'You can go, Graham. I can handle this.'

'Yes. Yes, sir!' Graham turned and left them, with a slightly regretful glance in Nicola's direction.

Nicola managed to retain her calm expression, while inwardly she seethed. Obviously the task she had set herself was going to be far more difficult than even she had imagined. Back in London, planning this situation, she had vaguely imagined that after his initial annoyance Jason Wilde might conceivably come to appreciate her presence, but apparently she had underestimated him. He was far more calculating than she had thought. Hard all through, like steel. And then she remembered Louise, and her own determination hardened to match his.

Even so, it was impossible not to appreciate the man himself. She could easily see why Louise had been so impossibly infatuated with him. He was so much different from George, or Michael either, for that matter. Not that she, personally, found his raw masculinity appealing. There was something primitive about him that stirred the basest emotions inside her, and she realized she would have to work hard to achieve any kind of victory with him. His height immediately put her at a disadvantage, and the width of his shoulders owed nothing to artifice. But it was the hard, uncompromising features, and the thick hair that grew low on his neck and was repeated in the brown muscularity of his arms and chest that gave one the impression of leashed virility, and brutal strength. She shivered suddenly, hoping this task she had set herself would never get out of hand. Somehow she had the feeling that if it did she would be unable to control it.

Then she chided herself. Was she such a coward? Was she to give up simply because the task was proving more complex? She must think of David and Goliath; or Samson and Delilah, her subconscious taunted her mockingly. A smile curved her mouth unwillingly, and then she saw his eyes darken angrily.

'What is amusing you, Miss King?' he asked, in a hard tone. 'I shouldn't have thought the prospect of several weeks under conditions intolerable to most women would appeal to a butterfly like yourself!'

'A butterfly?' she exclaimed, in annoyance. 'I'm no

butterfly. I have to work for my living.'

'Indeed?' Jason's expression was derisive. 'And how well do you know Sir Harold Mannering?'

Nicola stiffened. 'As well as any secretary knows her boss,' she replied.

'Is that so? Then how come you were able to persuade him to let you come out here? I mean – that's no mean achievement.'

'I don't like your insinuations, Mr. Wilde.'

'Don't you? How terrible!' he mocked her. 'But then a woman in your position hasn't much chance of retaliation, has she?'

Nicola's fingers stung across his cheek almost before she could prevent them, and Jason caught her wrist in a vice-like grip. 'Don't you ever dare to do that again!' he muttered savagely, 'or I may forget that whatever your designation I am a gentleman, and respond in kind!'

Nicola was trembling, and she wrenched her wrist away shakily. 'Then – then don't say things like that!' she snapped angrily. 'You've absolutely no evidence on which to base remarks of that sort!'

'Haven't I? Well, I have the evidence of my own eyes, and you're simply not the kind of woman to come out here for no reason.'

'I – I have a reason. I'm to help you – and keep an eye on Paul.'

'Very neat.' Jason turned away, walking to the drinks cabinet and selecting a bottle. After a stiff whisky, he said: 'Okay, we won't argue about your relationship with Harold. Quite frankly, I'm too tired to attempt to sort it all out. But I have my opinions. You wouldn't deny me them?'

Nicola did not reply, but merely shook her head. As her temper subsided she felt annoyed with herself. She rubbed her wrist that pained a little. This would never do. She couldn't have Jason Wilde imagining she was some kind of easy woman. That wasn't at all the image she wanted to create. And somehow no matter what his own morals might be she could not see him finding a woman like that attractive. No, somehow she had to assume a much less aggressive personality. But how? How?

She considered reverting to woman's oldest weapon, tears, but then decided against it. Somehow she didn't think they would wash with Jason Wilde either.

Now he said: 'Can I offer you a drink? It's the least I can do.'

Nicola bit her lip. 'Just a fruit juice, please,' she said quietly, and suffered the look of scorn that crossed his face before he turned and supplied her with an iced lime and lemon. Just then Ali appeared in the doorway, his huge dark eyes widening when he saw Nicola.

'Is there anything you want, sir?' he asked importantly, but Jason merely shook his head. However, Ali was not one to waste his opportunities, and he looked questioningly at Nicola as he said: 'Perhaps the lady would like something to eat, sir? Or has she already eaten?'

Jason's eyes darkened, and then, before he could reply, Nicola said: 'Why, how charming of your – er –

houseboy, Mr. Wilde. And how thoughtful, too. Particularly as you were so disappointed that I arrived late for dinner.'

Ali grinned. 'I will get the lady some curry and some fruit, yes?' he asked, looking at Jason. 'And perhaps some good coffee!'

Jason gave an exclamation, and then shrugged. 'Oh, do what you like,' he muttered broodingly, and Nicola hid a smile. She seemed to have scored at last.

'May I sit down?' she asked, subsiding on to a chair without waiting for his agreement. 'These are quite comfortable bungalows, aren't they? I mean – air-conditioning and so on. Not exactly what you'd expect to find in the middle of the desert.'

Jason leaned against the drinks cabinet, surveying her intently. 'Just what did you expect to find, Miss King?' he asked lazily.

Nicola sighed, and lay back in her chair. 'I thought we'd agreed to stop this baiting,' she said quietly. 'Have you travelled much, Mr. Wilde?'

'I imagine you would think so,' he returned broodingly. 'Have you?'

'Since coming to work for Sir Harold, yes,' she answered. 'We went to South America in March, and Trinidad in August. This is my first visit to the Middle East.'

'And what do you think of it?'

She shrugged. 'Primitive – but with definite possibilities.'

Jason shook his head. 'How old are you, Miss King?'

33

'I'm twenty-four, Mr. Wilde. How old are you?'

Jason was taken aback. 'Thirty-seven,' he replied shortly.

'And you've never got married?'

She saw a strange look cross his face. 'No,' he said slowly. 'How about you?'

Nicola sighed. 'I was engaged once. It was broken off a year ago.'

'Is that so? About the time you came to work for Sir Harold, in fact.'

'Sir Harold had nothing to do with my broken engagement,' she replied, rather shortly, and realized he didn't believe her.

However, Ali returned just then with a faultlessly laid tray containing a delicious-smelling dish of chicken curry, and another containing an assortment of citrus fruit. A jug of coffee completed the meal, and Nicola smiled at him gratefully.

She glanced at Jason. 'What is your man's name? I'd like to thank him.'

But Jason didn't have to answer. Ali was perfectly capable of doing that for himself. 'I am Ali, miss,' he said, bowing low. 'And it was my pleasure to prepare a meal for so beautiful a lady as yourself!'

Nicola smiled, offered her thanks, and then endeavouring to ignore Jason applied herself to the food. The curry was very hot, and Jason remarked, rather mockingly:

'Ali makes the food so hot that the climate seems cool by comparison.'

Nicola nodded, taking several gulps of the lime and

34

lemon to cool her mouth. However, it was very enjoyable, once she was used to the spiciness of it all, and she cleared her plate, and ate some grapes and an orange to finish. As she drank her coffee, Jason Wilde offered her a cigarette which she gratefully accepted.

'What are you going to give Paul to do?' she asked then.

Jason shrugged. 'I'm not sure. Something energetic, I think. To take a little of that pugnaciousness out of him!'

'You don't like him – why?'

'I neither like nor dislike him. He's merely an example of the futile waste of youth.'

Nicola lifted her shoulders. 'Were you never young?'

'Not as young as him, no!' Jason flung himself into a chair. 'As you're here, Harold says I have to use your – er – secretarial talents.'

'I know. I don't mind. I like working.'

'You amaze me. Who did you work for before you joined Inter-Anglia?'

'A small advertising company. I was the secretary there.'

Jason bent his head, digesting this information. Then he said: 'Anyway, as you are here, I think I ought to warn you that this is not England, and the customs of this country have, to a certain extent, to be adhered to.'

'What do you mean?' Nicola frowned.

'I mean that there are a number of Arabs working

on the site. Their encampment is beyond the camp. You'll see it in the morning. They live there with their wives and children. It's their normal life. They're naturally nomads. But their women are protected to a far greater degree than are ours. And you being here might cause a positive furore when the Sheikh gets to know.'

Nicola smiled. She couldn't take him seriously. 'The Sheikh,' she echoed softly. 'How romantic!'

Jason stared at her angrily. 'For heaven's sake, don't get any ideas in that direction! Sheikhs are not romantic figures of the mid-twenties movie screen. They are men, like other men, and most of them consider European women self-seeking and virtueless!'

Nicola's eyes widened. 'You certainly paint a very depressing picture, Mr. Wilde,' she remarked dryly. 'However, I can take care of myself, so I shouldn't worry unduly.'

'I don't,' muttered Jason vehemently. 'Believe me, my only anxieties concern the rig and the pipeline, not your person! What you do, and the outcome of your actions only concerns me in so far as they affect my schedule here.'

Nicola felt anger overtaking all other emotions. She had never met a man who was so infuriatingly indifferent to her.

'If you don't mind,' she said, getting to her feet, 'I should like to go to bed now!'

Jason rose too, regarding her with eyes that held a tinge of sardonic amusement. 'I should,' he replied, nodding. 'Tomorrow will be a long day. We rise here about five-thirty, and work starts at six-thirty. Think you can make it?'

His tone was derisive, and she stiffened. 'Oh, yes, Mr. Wilde,' she replied tautly, 'I can make it.'

'Good. I'll have Ali escort you back to Caxton's bungalow. At least I can't have Sir Harold accusing me of allowing you to wander unescorted about the camp!'

'That won't be necessary!' snapped Nicola, even as she knew she would not be able to distinguish which bungalow was hers. But her temper had got the better of her, and she could not restrain her retort.

Jason half-smiled, rather unpleasantly. 'Is that so?' he drawled. 'Okay. Good night, Miss King. Sleep well.'

Nicola stared at him. She ought to have known he would take every opportunity to humiliate her. Collecting her handbag, she walked to the door, but before she could pass through it, Jason said:

'Wait! I'll walk with you.'

Nicola stared at him, unwillingly aware that in other circumstances she would have found him very attractive. There was something about the huskiness of his voice and the lazy, panther-like way he moved that made her intensely conscious of him.

'Thank you,' was all she said now, and preceded him out of the door and down the steps to the packed sandy earth of the track.

They walked in silence, and when they reached her bungalow, he merely said 'Good night,' before walking silently away. Nicola watched him go, his hands thrust into the pockets of the close-fitting cream pants he was wearing, his dark head bent as he seemed deep in thought, and then she hastily ran up the steps and into the bungalow.

She shook off the feeling of apprehension that had suddenly engulfed her. This task she had set herself seemed suddenly frightening, and she realized it was a combination of the isolation, and the night, and the man himself that was responsible for her sudden indecision.

Her clothes were still in the two suitcases she had brought with her, but apart from drawing out a pair of nylon pyjamas, she didn't bother to unpack them, and after undressing merely cleaned her teeth before climbing wearily into the hard narrow bed. Actually, though, after a time, she realized the bed was quite comfortable, and the heat which had abated had left her glad of the warmth of the blankets. She snuggled her chin beneath the covers, and closed her eyes. But sleep was elusive. So many things had happened, and her mind buzzed with ideas and speculations, most of them centring on the man she had come out here to find, Jason Wilde.

Thinking of him brought thoughts of her sister Louise, and she wondered rather anxiously how she was getting along in the flat without her. Still, she had little Jane, and Tony, and the part-time job that Nicola had found for her. It was strange how Louise, six years her senior, should always arouse this feeling of responsibility inside her. Maybe it was because Louise always seemed so helpless, so totally incapable of fending for herself. That was why Nicola felt such anger towards Jason Wilde. He must have known how helpless, how defenceless, Louise was, and yet he had used every trick in the book to make her infatuated with him. Why couldn't he have chosen a woman more fitted to his personality? Someone who when discarded would not have fallen apart so completely.

Nicola rolled on to her stomach. Oh, yes, Jason Wilde had a lot to answer for, not least being the destruction of her own happiness. She punched her pillow. She would not think of it. She would not think of him. She had spent too many nights lying awake thinking of this affair.

An unearthly roar broke the stillness, and she sat up, sweating, staring into the darkness. What on earth had it been? Then she relaxed as realization came to her. Jason had said the Arabs were camped just outside the limits of the oil company's colony. Doubtless they would have camels. She had heard the noise camels could make in the streets of Gitana.

She lay back again, forcing her mind to be blank. But it was no good. Too many thoughts came to plague her. She wondered how long she would be forced to stay out here, how long she would be allowed to stay. Sir Harold had said he himself would come out later, to see how Paul was progressing, and to visit the local sheikh. This would be the man Jason Wilde had spoken of. Nicola wondered what manner of man he was. Might it be possible to use him in her efforts to discredit Jason Wilde?

It was much too early to tell. She would have to wait

and see. A good tactician never acted without being completely in possession of the facts of the situation. For the present she would do the job she had been employed to do and then. . . . She sighed. Anything might happen. And as a kind of bonus there was the undeniable excitement of life in this desert outpost. How could anyone sleep with so many possibilities before them?

# CHAPTER THREE

THE following morning Nicola awakened early, disturbed by the sound of someone banging on the mesh of her window. She slid tiredly out of bed, and peered round the thin curtains which she had drawn the night before. Graham Wilson's cheerful face gazed back at her.

'It's six o'clock,' he said, grinning. 'Jason said you'd want to be up and about.'

Nicola hid a grimace. 'He would,' she said, unable to prevent herself, and then smiled. 'Yes, thank you, Mr. Wilson. What do I do about breakfast?'

Graham put his hands on his hips. 'Jason said I was to take you to the canteen. He said the men would have to see you sooner or later, so it might as well be sooner.'

Nicola digested this. 'All right. Give me five minutes.'

Graham nodded, and in a little more than that time Nicola emerged looking smart and businesslike in the levis and a clean blouse, her hair caught up in a knot on top of her head.

'Hm!' murmured Graham appreciatively. 'That's what's been missing around here. I'd never have guessed!'

Nicola accepted his comments with a friendly smile. She liked Graham Wilson. There was something innately nice and honest about him. He wasn't much taller than she was, and had a broad stocky frame, his hair curly and gingery. He certainly presented no problems, and that was what she liked most.

In the brilliance of morning the small camp was dwarfed by the immense expanse of open country beyond the bungalows. Yesterday, driving in the car with Paul, Nicola had been too tense to take a great deal of pleasure in her surroundings, but now she felt a sense of humility as she gazed upon the vast stretches of sand-dunes rising to curiously stark rock formations, and the pale lilac line of the mountains beyond. The sky was incredible, the bluest blue she had ever seen, and the sand was a wonderful rich colour with a texture she had not felt before. It was not like any sand she had ever seen, but of course this was no shoreline, this was desert, raw and savage and untamed, dangerous to anyone without knowledge of its ever-changing personality.

Then she gave her attention to her immediate surroundings, the regimented lines of bungalows, the clubhouse, the general stores, the electricity generator; common everyday things that she was used to living beside. It was strange that there was no vegetation. Some scrub managed to survive in the shade of the buildings, but there were no trees, no flowering shrubs such as adorned gardens back home. There seemed to be no natural supply of water here and she wondered where the supply came from.

There were several groups of men making their way to the canteen this morning, and they stared without compunction at Nicola, obviously amazed that she should have suddenly appeared. Some of the men spoke to Graham, and he explained vaguely that she had been sent out by the oil company to expedite the delivery of Jason's paper work. There were some derisive stares at this piece of information, but most of the men seemed friendly enough, and after the initial sensation of being a peculiarity Nicola got used to their curiosity.

The canteen was a huge building, one end given over to a kind of bar, while the other served food of every variety. Nicola was amazed at the choice offered to her, but when Graham Wilson would have provided her with cereal, bacon, eggs, toast and coffee, she hastily demurred. She could only manage toast and coffee at this hour of the morning.

They found a table and sat down, and Graham said: 'You'll notice not all the men are English here. There are Italians, and French, as well as one or two other nationalities. When the papers are delivered it's like an international convention.'

Nicola's eyes widened. 'You get papers?' she exclaimed.

Graham grinned wryly. 'They're several days old by the time we get our hands on them. Still, it's nice to keep up to date with the gossip.'

'And where is your home?' asked Nicola, buttering a slice of toast as she spoke.

'In Birmingham. Didn't you guess? Jason says the accent is inches thick!'

Nicola smiled. 'No, I didn't guess, although now you

mention it . . .' They both laughed, and immediately attracted the attention of the whole room. Nicola was surprised to find herself flushing. She had thought she was past such things.

As the meal progressed, Graham told her quite a lot about the organization at Castanya. Apparently Jason Wilde was the senior engineer on the site, and well versed in the troubles such enterprises could come up against.

'Ian Mackenzie is in charge of the actual field,' Graham continued, 'and Jason's out in the desert, supervising the pipeline, keeping it moving towards the sea.'

'How much further does it have to go?' Nicola asked. 'Will it take much longer to complete it?'

'About nine or ten months,' answered Graham. 'There are two hundred and sixty miles between Castanya and the seaport of Gitana. We've covered about sixty miles so far.'

'And it will take so long to complete it?'

'Sure. The pipes are in lengths of between twenty and forty feet and need to be welded together on the spot. That, combined with sand-storms, precarious working conditions and the rest, can make for pretty slow development.'

'Do you have to bury the pipes?'

'Well, it hardly seems sensible. Sand is a great mover, and a sand-storm can shift tons of sand from one area to another. A pipeline buried today could be exposed tomorrow. Consequently they have to be properly protected against corrosion. Then there are the pumping stations to be built. Obviously oil needs constant propulsion to keep it moving, and the pumping station here at Castanya wouldn't have the power to push the oil over sand-dunes and across such a tremendous distance.'

'I see.' Nicola was impressed. 'So that is what Mr. Wilde is accomplishing.'

'Among other things, yes. He's also having problems with the Sheikh. He doesn't think the men we're using – his men, that is – are getting paid enough. So Jason's increased their percentage.'

'It's quite a complex affair, isn't it? I never realized.' Nicola finished her coffee and accepted a cigarette from Graham. 'Is the field producing oil at the moment?'

'Oh, yes. But it's being stored in the main. Some has been sent down the pipeline already completed to the next station at Isthali. They have a storage tank there, bigger than the one here.'

'And don't you get bored? I mean – what do you do during your leisure hours?'

'Well, various things. We play cards, read, write letters home, that sort of thing. And there's the pool, and the tennis court if you feel really energetic. There's even a cinema of a kind. It's run by two of the men, and from time to time they give a show.'

Nicola nodded. 'I suppose it's like an army camp, really.'

'I suppose it is. We're more or less self-sufficient here. Sometimes one or two of the men drive into Gitana, but mostly we mess about here. Swimming is the most enjoyable pastime.'

'Yes, but where does the water come from?' exclaimed Nicola interestedly.

'Oh, there's an oasis, not too far from here. We've run a pipeline from there. Naturally, the water needs purifying, but there's plenty of it.'

'I see.' Nicola bent her head. 'What am I to do today? Do you know? Have you seen Mr. Wilde?'

Graham shrugged. 'Not this morning. I'd hazard a guess that he's a good many miles out along the pipeline already.'

'Oh! You mean he's gone?'

'Yes. You're left in my charge,' grinned Graham. 'I'm to show you around, introduce you to the men, supply you with information, and eventually set you to work.' He looked apologetic.

'But what about Paul?' asked Nicola. 'Where's he?'

'With Jason,' replied Graham, pushing back his chair. 'Don't worry about your friend Mannering. He'll survive!'

'I'm not worried,' protested Nicola, but she did feel a slight sense of pique that Jason Wilde should abandon her so carelessly to the care of his second-in-command. He was obviously showing her in the most blatant way possible that she need expect no assistance from him.

During the next few days Nicola caught only glimpses of Jason Wilde moving about the camp. During the day he was out supervising the men and in the evenings, when dinner was over, Nicola was so exhausted she just felt like tumbling into bed. The days

46

were long for her, and the unaccustomed heat of the climate was enervating.

In addition to this she had found that there was indeed plenty of work for her in the office building. Two or three men worked there from time to time, but mostly she had the place to herself, and it was she who answered the telephone calls from the out-stations and from Gitana itself. She became quite conversant with the way they worked and was soon capable of deciding for herself what needed attending to. If Jason Wilde found her ministrations helpful he certainly never said anything, and as he shunned the offices when she was there she never knew whether he appreciated her efforts on his behalf.

After work was over, she usually finished about two when the heat was unbearably oppressive, she had her personal washing to attend to and as she needed to change her clothes sometimes twice or three times every day, she was kept busily employed.

Paul came to see her one evening when she was in her bungalow, stretched out in a chair, reading one of the thrillers she had found on the shelves in the living room. He looked tireder than she remembered, and possibly even a bit thinner, his eyes strained with fatigue.

'Hi,' he said, dropping into a chair opposite her, and offering her a cigarette.

Nicola accepted the cigarette, and then after it was lit, she said: 'You look worn out. Is Jason Wilde working you hard?'

Paul gave an expressive grimace. 'Is he not!' he exclaimed. 'Of course, he says it's just an ordinary day's work and I'm so out of condition living the kind of life I lived in London that I can't take it. Maybe he's right. I just know I'm beat!'

'Me, too,' said Nicola sympathetically. 'It's the heat, you know. Have you been okay? I mean – no stomach upsets, or anything.'

'Well, I felt a bit sick yesterday, but I'm better today.'

Nicola got up and lifted her handbag. 'Here,' she said, handing him two pills, 'take these when you go to bed. They're jolly good. I've not felt a twinge of discomfort, and I must admit the food is different from what I'm used to.'

Paul nodded. 'That's for sure,' he said gloomily. 'How about you? Are you working hard?'

Nicola shrugged and smiled. 'I guess so. But like you I'm tired all the time. Still, that will go in time. It's only a matter of getting acclimatized.'

'How long do you think Dad intends to keep me out here?' asked Paul, frowning.

Nicola's eyes widened. 'You didn't have to come,' she reminded him dryly.

'What was the alternative?' asked Paul. 'Being cut off without a penny and having to get a job in England. No, thanks! If I have to get a job I'd rather it was out of England, away from all the people I know.'

'I see. Still, you could have got a job independently of your father.'

'No, I couldn't.' Paul shook his head. 'Don't you know, I'm the world's weakest character!' His tone was

48

sardonic. 'If I know it, I guess everyone else knows it too!'

'Don't be such a defeatist!' she exclaimed. 'Your father's not so frightening.'

'Not to you, maybe. No, I just go with the tide.'

Nicola walked to the kitchen door. 'Want some coffee? I've mastered the art of making that at least,' she laughed.

'Couldn't you? Before?' Paul looked astonished.

'Oh, of course! That was a joke!' she said exasperatedly. 'Honestly, Paul, I think you're losing your sense of humour as well as everything else.'

Paul hunched his shoulders. 'Well, I would like some coffee. Thanks!'

'So would I!' remarked a lazy voice, and Nicola swung round to find Jason Wilde there, leaning against the door post. How long had he been there? Listening to their conversation!

Nicola stifled her annoyance. This was the first she had seen of him for days, and she couldn't afford to waste her opportunities.

'All right,' she said, brushing past him, on her way to the kitchen. She was supremely conscious of him, and she half-felt that he knew it. That would never do. No matter how eager she might be, he must make all the running. But would he?

She heard their voices in the lounge as she made the coffee in the tiny kitchen at the back of the bungalow. She wondered what they were saying to one another, and her fingers fumbled with her impatience to get back.

However, when she did return, the tray laden with three cups and the coffee jug, Paul was gone. She looked round in surprise, and Jason Wilde turned from his contemplation of a print Caxton had hung on the stark wall of the living room.

'Paul decided he needed his sleep more than coffee,' he said lazily. 'Put that tray down. Before you drop it!'

Nicola compressed her lips and stood down the tray on the low table in the centre of the floor. She didn't know whether to be glad or sorry that Paul had gone. True she was glad Jason Wilde had stayed, but somehow she didn't think the reason he had stayed was a complimentary one.

'Cream and sugar?' she asked, in a taut little voice, seating herself beside the tray, and wishing he would sit down. He was too overpowering standing there before her like some restless animal.

'Thank you, no.' Jason shook his head. 'I'd prefer something a little more stimulating than coffee. Do you mind if I help myself?'

Nicola felt furious; she might as well have saved her energies if she was going to have to drink a whole jug of coffee herself.

'Go ahead!' she said now, disguising her annoyance, and poured herself some coffee and began to sip it jerkily.

Jason poured himself a stiff measure of whisky, and then seated himself opposite her. His eyes surveyed her appraisingly, making her self-consciously aware that she had not washed since dinner, and her face felt greasy and unattractive. She was still wearing levis, as she had found the men took less notice of her if she dressed in casual clothes, and her hair, once immaculately combed into a topknot, straggled a little about the nape of her neck. Brushing back some wisps of hair, she said:

'To what do I owe the honour of this visit?'

Jason studied the drink in his hand, giving her a chance to look at him without his being aware of it. In dark brown slacks and a cream knitted cotton shirt, open almost to his waist, he looked disturbingly male, and Nicola looked away from him, annoyed with herself for dwelling on him.

Finally, he said: 'I don't want Paul Mannering visiting you here, alone.'

Nicola's head jerked up. 'What is that supposed to mean?'

'Exactly what it says – I don't want him coming here.'

Nicola's temper got out of control. 'Just who the hell do you think you are?' she exclaimed angrily. 'Dictating who or who may not come here!' She took a gulp of air. 'While I live in this bungalow it's my property, and I say who does or does not come in!'

'No, you don't,' he replied quietly, dangerously quietly had she been calm enough to become aware of it. 'I am the boss around here, and I say what goes. This bungalow belongs to the oil company, and is always their property. Besides which, so long as I am in charge here, you will not go around acting like some amateur *femme fatale*!'

51

'How – how dare you!' Nicola almost choked on the words.

'I dare because there are a group of men here, under my control, who have the idea that what goes for one, goes for all! What do you imagine would happen if it became generally known that Paul Mannering was a regular visitor here? What do you suppose would be the reactions of the men? Do you think perhaps they might conceivably get the wrong idea about you? Or that they'd resent the fact of Paul getting such favourable treatment? Do you think they'll demand the right to bring out their own wives, or girl-friends?'

Nicola was silent, hating him for his cold logical brain. 'Paul is a friend,' she ventured at last.

'And what is Graham Wilson?'

'What do you mean?'

'Only that Wilson is neglecting his own work to keep around you. He's already rousing comment by the way he continually sits with you at meals.'

'I can't help that,' she flared.

'Yes, you can. You could eat alone. Or bring your food back here.'

'What! Carry it across that dusty track to the bungalow!' Nicola was horrified. 'It would be cold, and dusty as anything!'

'Then try and behave more circumspectly!' said Jason flatly. 'I know that's asking a lot of a woman like you, but at least try.'

Nicola's colour deepened and she got to her feet abruptly. 'I think you're despicable!' she exclaimed, all ideas of remaining calm flying out of the window in that moment. 'You can't come here and tell me how to act! You're not God, you know! You're just a man, like other men! And I'm not your slave, and nor is Paul!'

Jason Wilde got to his feet. 'Did Paul say I was treating him like a slave?' he asked ominously.

'Yes! No! That is – oh, I don't know! You're getting me so confused I don't know what I'm saying!' Nicola turned away.

'And do you think I treat you like a slave?' he asked quietly.

Nicola shrugged, bending her head. 'No, I suppose not,' she said grudgingly.

'You certainly don't seem to have taken any harm from your first week here anyway,' he remarked dryly. Then he walked to the door. 'Thanks for the company while I drank. I can hardly thank you for the drink, can I?'

Nicola did not reply, and he halted in the doorway.

'By the way,' he said, 'I'm driving to Umbyra tomorrow. Want to come?'

'Umbyra?' Nicola swung round. 'Where's that?'

'Inland. Some fifty odd miles. It's a courtesy visit to one of the Bedouin chiefs. I thought you might like to come along.'

Nicola stared at him. It hardly seemed possible that only five minutes before he had been berating her for entertaining Paul in the bungalow, so relaxed did he now seem. She couldn't resist the dig that rose to her lips.

'Are you not afraid the men will imagine I'm favouring you with my attentions?' she asked mockingly.

Jason Wilde gave her a derisive smile. 'They know me better than that,' he remarked wryly. 'Besides, I want to take some readings on the way. You can make yourself useful.'

Nicola shrugged her slim shoulders. 'I thought there would be a catch,' she remarked coldly.

'No catch,' he answered. 'Well?'

Nicola lifted her shoulders again. 'What about the office?'

'Graham can spend his time there. Do you want to come or don't you?'

'I – well, of course.'

'Good. We leave at six. I'll have some sandwiches packed so that we won't have to wait for breakfast.'

Nicola glanced at her watch. It was already after ten o'clock. That meant that she could expect between six and seven hours' sleep at the very most, and somehow in this climate that just wasn't enough. But she nodded, and he, sensing her desire to get to bed, wished her good night and disappeared down the steps.

After he had gone, she went hastily into the bathroom and showered, before sliding beneath the covers. Excitement tingled along every inch of her being. Tomorrow she was to have a wonderful chance of being alone with Jason Wilde. Somehow she must quell the anger and hatred she felt towards him, and endeavour to appear to him as a young and attractive woman. After all, he was only a man. She must succeed.

She was awake at five, when the first fingers of light

54

began to tinge the sky, and was dressed and waiting on the verandah when she saw a Land-Rover churning up the dust on its way to her bungalow. She stood up, aware of a trembling sensation in her knees, and wondered why Jason Wilde should disturb her so. It must be because of her foreknowledge of the reasons she was setting out to attract him, but even so, there was something about him that challenged her persistently to prove his vulnerability.

He halted at the steps, and thrust open the vehicle's nearside door. She ran down the steps, slid into the Land-Rover, and slammed the door. The site was just coming to life, but no one took any notice of the Land-Rover or its occupants, it was much too early in the day.

They left the site by the southern route, heading out into limitless wastes of sand. Nicola, glancing at her travelling companion, wondered at the indifference he showed towards such empty spaces. Didn't it disturb him at all that a sand-storm could obliterate all traces of a route previously well defined, so that a traveller might lose his way for ever in these endless rolling dunes?

She saw the encampment of the Arabs, the horses and camels lying outside the perimeter tents, raising their eyes in bored speculation. The sun was getting hotter, and with the windows closed, it began to get humid in the small compartment.

'You realize why I wanted to travel in the early hours,' Jason remarked, speaking for the first time. 'It can get unbearably hot later in the day.'

Nicola fanned herself. 'It's pretty hot now,' she replied, smoothing her hair behind her ears. She had left it loose, it was more becoming that way, but it lay heavily on her neck so that she longed to put it up. The bandanna she had tied around it would soon dampen with the heat and then her hair would feel lank and lifeless. Perhaps she would have been better succumbing to coolness rather than appearance.

Jason seemed aware of her discomfort, for he said: 'Long hair isn't particularly practical in this climate.'

Nicola quelled the ready retort that rose to her lips. 'I like my hair long,' she said evenly.

'I'm sure you do,' he agreed lazily, swinging the wheel through his lean brown hands. 'I was merely stating the obvious.'

Nicola watched his hands on the wheel, his wrists with the dark hairs that grew on them, the thick gold band of his watch, a heavy gold signet ring on his little finger.

'Tell me,' she said probingly, 'what part of England do you come from?'

'Well, my parents come from Yorkshire, but settled near London several years ago,' he replied easily. 'My father is retired now, and they live in Worthing.'

'I see. Do you have any relatives – I mean brothers or sisters?'

Jason shrugged. 'Two sisters. Both married. Both older than I am.' His reply was slightly less responsive, as though he didn't particularly care for such questioning. Nevertheless, Nicola had to go on.

'Haven't you ever thought of getting married, Mr. Wilde?' she asked, looking sideways at him.

Jason felt in his breast pocket for his cigarettes, and getting them out dropped them into her lap. 'Light two,' he said briefly. 'Perhaps that will give you something to think about instead of me!'

Nicola grew hot with embarrassment. He had the knack of reducing her to a disconcerted teenager by his brash remarks. So she lit two cigarettes, and passed one to him which he glanced at before putting it between his lips.

'Good,' he said. 'You haven't smothered it with lipstick.'

Nicola breathed deeply. 'I'm not wearing any make-up,' she said tautly.

'Aren't you?' He glanced her way. 'That's a refreshing change.'

'What do you mean?'

'Oh, nothing personal, I can assure you. However, I can't remember the last time I saw a girl without make-up. It suits you.'

'Thank you.' Nicola almost choked on the words, and then gave her attention to smoking, and tried to forget her companion for a few cooling minutes. But it was difficult when she was conscious of him with every fibre of her being.

She concentrated on the barren landscape until her eyes ached behind her dark glasses. It was such a strain endeavouring to distinguish something, some landmark, with which to identify their passage. Outcrops of rock were nondescript, although she supposed that

Jason might recognize their characteristics.

When she saw a cluster of date palms in the far distance she thought she was seeing things, and glanced surreptitiously at Jason to see whether he showed any reaction at all. He intercepted her glance, and half-smiled.

'Don't alarm yourself,' he remarked laconically. 'Didn't Graham tell you about Lezzani?'

Nicola hesitated. 'The oasis?' she questioned.

'That's right.'

'Oh, then yes, he did. For a minute I thought I was seeing a mirage.'

Jason swung the Land-Rover across the track and made a direct course for the oasis. When they were close by, he said: 'We'll stop for a while and eat. If we leave the Rover open it will circulate the air. We've still some distance to go to Umbyra.'

Nicola was more than willing, although her stomach plunged a little at the thought of a meal *à deux* with him. She deliberately brought Louise's wan little face to mind, and immediately her resolution hardened. He had shown no pity, why should she? Only her uneasy lack of confidence troubled her now.

The meal Ali had prepared was more than adequate, but Nicola had only one sandwich, an orange and some coffee while Jason Wilde ate bacon rolls, egg patties, and drank several cups of coffee while he pored over some maps he had laid across his knees. He had set the hamper beneath the palms where Nicola had an enchanting view of the wide pool that formed the oasis. Reeds edged its perimeter and she thought how marvellous it would have been to bathe in really cool water. But of course, she couldn't, so she sat beneath the trees and watched Jason, wishing she had some miraculous method of drawing his attention to herself. But short of creating some kind of disturbance there seemed nothing would disturb the quiet of the place and its absolute isolation. She had never experienced such stillness, with not even a bird or an animal to provide distraction. There were plenty of insects, of course, and she was constantly brushing them from her bare arms where she had rolled back the sleeves of her shirt, but otherwise all was calm.

At last she got to her feet and walked to the water's edge, staring down into its depths with some amazement. It was startling really that water could appear here, miles from anywhere, without any apparent source.

'What's wrong?' asked a voice behind her. 'Bored?'

Nicola looked round. Jason was still lounging beneath the palms, but he had put his maps away. 'Yes,' she said, deciding to be honest. 'Must you constantly work? Don't you ever relax? I mean – the men on the site have their free time. I haven't noticed you having any leave since I arrived.'

'Did you really notice?' he murmured, rather derisively, and she turned her back on him again, unwilling to give him the satisfaction of knowing he had embarrassed her again.

'Tell me something,' he murmured suddenly. 'Just why did you come out here, Miss King?'

Nicola controlled an involuntary start. 'You know that as well as I do,' she replied calmly. 'Is it such a novelty? Having feminine companionship?'

'Not at all. In fact women are no longer the trembling vines they used to be. I know of women geologists, scientists; I guess it's conceivable that there are women engineers. It's just that usually women who are forced to work with men are – shall we say – less decorative, in the main. That still doesn't alter my opinion, of course, that Harold Mannering sent you out here for some nefarious purposes of his own.'

'That's ridiculous!' exclaimed Nicola sharply. 'But at least Sir Harold is a human being – not a machine! He reacts to emotional impulses as well as physical ones.'

'What's that supposed to mean? That I'm a machine? That I don't have emotional impulses?'

Nicola compressed her lips. 'Oh, you have emotional impulses, all right,' she replied coldly. 'But like everything else in your life, they're categorized!'

'What do you know about my life?' Jason's eyes narrowed. 'We only met a few days ago. How could you possibly know anything about me?'

Nicola flushed. 'I've read about you – in reports,' she said, breathing a deep sigh as the lie came easily to her.

Jason looked sceptical, but after glancing at his watch he got to his feet. 'Come on, let's go. I want to be at Umbyra by eight.'

'Eight?' murmured Nicola, almost to herself. Was it really only an hour since they had set off? It seemed much longer than that.

The Land-Rover had had time to cool down in the shade of the date palms and Nicola was quite glad to be on the way again. Arguments with Jason Wilde tended to get a little out of hand, and she had the feeling that in a genuine encounter she would not stand much chance of bettering him. Considering it was already a year since Louise's breakdown she was still ridiculously emotional about the whole business, and that must account for the ease with which Jason Wilde was capable of upsetting her. Even so, since getting to know him she had to admit he possessed a compelling personality, and the forthrightness of his questions did much to disconcert her. From Louise's description she had expected a much less disturbing presence. Of course, she had expected him to be attractive, Louise had been very explicit in that direction, but it was something else, some purely sensuous reaction he produced in herself, that frightened her a little. She had thought she knew almost everything there was to know about men.

Jason glanced at her, noticing her pensive expression. 'Is something troubling you?' he asked curiously.

Nicola started. 'No. No, of course not. Why should there be?' she exclaimed. 'I was thinking about something, that's all, something private.'

Jason shrugged. 'Pardon me for intruding,' he remarked sardonically, and Nicola realized she had been indiscreet again. If she was to get anywhere with this man she must stop behaving like a shrew.

'I'm sorry,' she said now, managing a frank smile. 'Tell me about these readings you have to take. What are they?'

Jason studied her for a moment, as though gauging why his words should have produced so unexpected a reaction, and then began to tell her, rather expressionlessly, about the search for oil, and its accompanying techniques. He told her about gravity meters, and magnetometers, and seismographs, describing their particular uses in detail, until she was lost in scientific data. She thought he had done it deliberately, but she refrained from telling him so. Instead, she showed an intense interest, and after a while he was disarmed and warmth crept back into his voice, and she realized he really enjoyed his work.

They stopped once in their passage across a vast expanse of rocklike strata, slightly different from the softer surface of impacted sand, and Nicola perched on her seat, her legs dangling, watching Jason as he extracted a strange instrument from the back of the Land-Rover and set it down on the rocky ground. Restraining the impulse to ask what it was, she waited, and presently he indicated that she should come and look into it as he was doing.

Nicola slid off her seat and jumped to the ground. She approached him cautiously, unsure as to whether this was some trick he was playing on her. But it was not, and she read the gauges as he had done, and listened as he explained the uses of the gravity meter they were using.

'This is geophysics,' he remarked later, as he returned the machine to the Land-Rover. 'Measuring the gravitational force of the earth. Obviously the gravitational pull is not the same at all points, and a more solid formation below ground indicates possible masses of rock. It's possible with the use of a seismograph to set up impulses in the ground, so that when they're measured on a seismograph it can be calculated whether there are folds in the rock where oil might be trapped.'

Nicola climbed into her seat. 'It's interesting,' she agreed, finding she really was enjoying learning about his work. 'I suppose most people imagine an oil company just drills and drills until they strike oil.'

Jason smiled. 'Drilling's a pretty expensive business,' he remarked. 'Apart from which it wastes a hell of a lot of time. No one can ever be absolutely certain of the presence of oil. It's just that some places are more possible than others. It's up to the geo-physicist to find these places.'

'Is that your job?'

'Hell, no! That's a job for an expert. It's not my field. Mine is all oil, and pipelines, and some liaison.'

Nicola frowned. 'You were offered a seat on the board. Why didn't you take it?' She had hoped he would, back in England, with no immediate possibility at that time of meeting him.

Jason shrugged his broad shoulders, and drew out his cigarettes again, flicking them into her lap, with a half smile, so that she knew he wanted her to light one for him again. 'It wasn't convenient,' he said now, making her jerk her head up to look at him sharply. 'I preferred to be out of the country.'

Nicola's fingers were all thumbs, and she hoped he wouldn't notice. 'Why?' she asked casually.

Jason accepted the cigarette she had lit, and drew on it deeply. 'For someone who usually treats me to scorn and derision, Miss King, you're inordinately interested in my affairs,' he remarked.

Nicola gasped. 'Not at all,' she snapped, and then got herself in check again. 'In-interested – that's all!'

'Okay. Then tell me something about yourself. I'm interested, too.' But she felt he wasn't, he was merely baiting her.

'What do you want to know?' she asked, lightly.

'Oh, the usual things. Background, hobbies, family! You know the sort of thing.'

Nicola sighed. 'You know my background. I'm Sir Harold's secretary, or at least I was.'

'Yes, that's what puzzles me,' said Jason thoughtfully. 'If you were Sir Harold's secretary, how come he let you come out here? I mean – why you, in particular?'

Nicola ran her tongue over her lips. 'I – I persuaded him,' she said frankly.

'I wonder how,' murmured Jason significantly.

Nicola decided to ignore this. If she began arguing with him again, she might get herself into more difficulties.

However, Jason wasn't finished. 'You said you were going to get married,' he said. 'What happened?'

Nicola compressed her lips. 'I'd rather not talk about it.'

'Sorry.' But he didn't sound it, and she wrinkled her nose.

The Land-Rover was nearing a kind of village now. Nicola could see houses, and smoke, and as they got nearer she could see a kind of fortified dwelling which Jason told her was the chief's residence.

'In the days when the tribes were fighting amongst themselves, it was always desirable to have one's house fortified,' he said. 'Can you see the crenellated watch-towers at the corners, the battlements?' He smiled. 'A fort, in fact.'

Nicola stared in amazement. Standing there with its backdrop of sky and palm trees, it was incredibly unreal, and the brilliance of the sun reflected on mud walls threw back its own reflection, blinding her with its brightness.

They drove between the huts of the villagers, some of whom came out to stand staring at them, the women holding their robes across their faces so that only the darkness of eyes could be seen. There were dozens of children, with bright inquisitive eyes, who seemed to find the sight of Nicola, with her honey-gold hair, quite startlingly interesting.

Jason smiled at her again, drawing a smile in return. 'Like I once said, you've come to a strange place with your appearance.'

'Why?'

'Well, you're so – English. I don't know, there's something about an English complexion, even one as tanned as yours. You've really surprised me, actually. With your colouring I should have thought the sun would burn your skin, but it hasn't. It suits you.'

That was better! Nicola's eyes held his for a moment, deliberately, and a strange questing glance appeared in the depths of his before he withdrew his gaze, leaving her peculiarly enervated suddenly.

They stopped in the courtyard of the fort. Now Nicola could see it was in a sad state of neglect, and the heavy gates that had once protected it now hung on weak hinges, and obviously were never closed. At Jason's indication, she slid out when he did, and followed him to the entrance, and through the doorway into a shadowy hall. The darkness after the brilliance outside was unnerving, and Nicola hovered near the doorway, unwilling to advance into darkness that was both weird and pungently aromatic.

Jason turned, and a hand caught her wrist in a firm hold. 'Don't be alarmed,' he remarked, drawing her towards him. 'No one is going to hurt you.'

Nicola stifled a retort. 'It's rather – well, smelly,' she murmured uncomfortably, and Jason laughed.

'Yes, isn't it? However, you'll soon get used to that. Come on. Mustafa will know we have arrived by now. He will wonder what's delaying us.'

Nicola had to go with him or brave a lonely vigil outside with a crowd of curious tribesmen and women. But, as they traversed the empty corridors, and she began to see vaguely again, she felt an awful sense of nausea. The smell of disuse and decay and unwashed bodies was overpowering, and she wondered how she would bear spending any length of time in such a place.

But when they reached the chamber where a huge Arab was squatting on the floor waiting for them, she found the odour alleviated by another, more potent scent of something that repelled as well as appealed. It was not pleasant, and yet it was not unpleasant, and her head swam dizzily for a few moments, so that the opulence of this chamber almost passed her by. But as her senses cleared she saw the rich tapestries hanging on the walls, and admired the richness of the ornamentation. The room was in the inner recesses of the building, and there was no daylight, only light from lamps hanging from the ceiling which also was intricately carved.

Jason greeted their host, introduced Nicola, and then indicated that she should do as he did and sit on the floor, only behind him.

Nicola objected to this, but decided she might as well obey as cause another argument, and while the two men talked, she took in the strange scene. Standing behind the fat Mustafa were two women, with huge palm leaves which they waved languidly, causing a pleasing draught to encompass the bulk of their master. He really was enormous, with massive, fleshy fingers, covered with rings that sparkled in the artificial light. Nicola wondered why he didn't use some of his obvious wealth to improve his surroundings. She glanced at Jason. Beside Mustafa he looked tall and lean and very dark. She wondered how he would look in Eastern dress. She thought he might suit the white robes and flowing headdress. Then she squashed the thought.

Jason Wilde looked right as he was, in his levis and cotton shirt. He needed nothing to make him even more sure of himself. He had superb self-confidence.

Eventually, after talk, wine was served, and Nicola was allowed a glass. She sniffed the beverage she was offered rather suspiciously, but Jason merely moved his head slightly, indicating that she should drink it. She did so, and found it rather too sweet for her taste. Then it was time to leave.

However, Mustafa now turned his attention to Nicola, and made some remark about her to Jason. As the whole of their conversation had been incomprehensible to Nicola, she objected to herself becoming a subject for discussion, and felt an infuriated sense of frustration as Jason said something that made Mustafa roar with laughter and make eloquent gestures with his hands. Nicola looked hard at Jason, and said in a tight little voice:

'Are you ready to leave?'

Jason nodded, and Mustafa struggled to his feet. He came across to her, walking round her rather disconcertingly, and then he touched the gold of her hair with his flabby fingers. Nicola cringed inwardly, but Jason's eyes were hard and steady as he stared at her and she made no objection. Then Mustafa said something else, for which Jason had no ready retort. Instead he shook his head and taking Nicola's arm guided her to the door, where good-byes were said. Nicola managed a faint smile, and then they were walking back along the corridors towards the welcoming daylight outside.

Jason said nothing until they were in the Land-

Rover, and then he said: 'You really will have to harden yourself to this kind of thing if you intend to stay here,' in a cold voice.

'What do you mean?' Nicola's breath came in jerky gasps.

Jason swung the Land-Rover round in a half-circle and headed back through the village. 'You're too squeamish,' he said coldly. 'If you imagined the desert as some kind of technicolor epic where nothing repels, nothing hurts, nothing is unpleasant, you were sadly mistaken.'

Nicola stared at him. 'I didn't imagine any such thing. As for – for – for that – in there,' she glanced back, 'I don't like any man pawing me.'

'Mustafa wasn't pawing you! He was admiring you!' snapped Jason.

'I suppose he wanted to buy me for his harem!' she said sarcastically.

Jason uttered an expletive. 'You!' He shook his head. 'You're much too scrawny for Mustafa!'

'I'm not scrawny!' Nicola was horrified.

'He thinks so. He thinks your hair is pretty, though.'

'Thank you!' Nicola stared out of the car's windows. 'Anyway, I'm glad it's over.'

'So am I. Now we can take our time getting back.'

Nicola blinked. 'What time is it? My watch seems to have stopped.'

'Half after eleven,' replied Jason briefly. 'We'll be back at the oasis before one. We'll have lunch there and return to the camp this afternoon.'

'Lunch?' echoed Nicola. 'But have you brought lunch, too?'

'Ali packed enough for half a dozen meals,' replied Jason smoothly. 'Why? Do you want to go straight back?'

'No!' Nicola flushed. 'That is – well, won't your men wonder where you are? Where I am?'

'Probably. However, I think we can comfortably forget them for an hour or so, don't you?'

Nicola was doubtful. Somehow now she wished they were going straight back to the camp. She had wanted to attract Jason Wilde, indeed that was her first objective, but it was one thing to plan something cold-bloodedly back in England, and quite another to carry that something out when the man involved had such an annoying way of disconcerting her.

Still, she must not think of herself. She must think of Louise, and the children, and the havoc he had wrought in her own affairs.

The oasis was a beautiful sight after so much barrenness. Nicola slid out of the Land-Rover, and ran to the water's edge, dipping her handkerchief into the water and wiping her hot cheeks. It was remarkably cool, and she knelt down beside it, allowing her wrists to rest under the coolness. Soon the blood circulated that coolness to all parts of her body, and she sighed, and wiped her hands on the sides of her pants. Then she looked round. Jason had taken a hamper out of the vehicle, and had set it down on a rug under the palms. He was now stretched out beside it, smoking a cigarette lazily. The heat didn't seem to affect him at all, except that he, like everyone else, sweated a good deal. Right now, he had loosened his shirt, and pulled it free of his pants for coolness.

Nicola walked across to him, and stood looking down at him a trifle nervously. His eyes flickered. 'Sit down,' he said. 'I promise I won't grab you or anything.'

Nicola hastily subsided on to the rug before he noticed her expression, opening the hamper and peering inside. Ali had certainly prepared a delicious picnic. There was salad, and ham, bread rolls, mayonnaise, little Eastern pastries simply oozing with nuts and a kind of sticky sweet filling, fresh fruit, and beer or lager.

'I'm sorry there's nothing hot to drink,' remarked Jason, propping himself on one elbow to watch her, 'but Ali thinks that everyone should drink long cool drinks this side of the Med.'

Nicola smiled. 'That's all right. I like lager,' she replied quickly. 'Shall I deal with the food?'

'Why not?' Jason lay back again. 'You know, you remind me of someone.'

Nicola's heart plunged. 'Oh,' she said casually. 'Who?'

Jason frowned thoughtfully. 'A girl – a girl I knew back in England. She wasn't much like you at all to look at – she was much smaller and less – *aggressive*!' He grinned. 'But there were certain characteristics she possessed that you possess, too.'

Nicola's hands were clammy, and a trifle unsteady. 'Wh – what was her name?' she queried lightly.

Jason looked at her intently. 'Now why should you want to know some strange girl's name?' he asked.

Nicola shrugged. 'No reason. Don't tell me. I don't care.'

Jason chewed his lips for a moment. 'Okay, her name was Louise, Louise Ellison. Do you know her?'

Nicola's colour nearly gave her away, but by an immense effort of will-power she restrained herself. 'Heavens, no!' she exclaimed. 'Why should I?'

Jason sat up, studying her with uncomfortable intensity. 'Because, you see, I happen to know she had a sister. Oh, I didn't meet her, or anything like that, but her name was Nicola, too. Now isn't that a coincidence?'

# CHAPTER FOUR

NICOLA was speechless. She didn't know what to say. She had already denied all knowledge of Louise Ellison and yet she had the feeling that Jason Wilde did not really believe her. What possible reason could she have had for denying such a thing? What plausible excuse could she think up? How could she be certain that his knowledge of her was no greater than she assumed? Had he tackled Sir Harold about her? Did he know in truth that she was related to Louise? The questions went round and round in her brain until she felt sick. Jason was still watching her, a half-smile playing round his lips, and she wondered if he fully realized what a furore he had plunged her into.

Toying with a plastic container containing bread rolls, Nicola said: 'What has that to do with me?' rather tentatively.

Jason shrugged. 'You tell me.'

Nicola clenched her fists. She felt furiously angry suddenly. How dared he sit there laughing at her confusion? Why didn't he come out into the open? If he knew she was Louise's sister, why didn't he say so? She heaved a sigh, and opened the container. 'Do you want some ham and salad rolls, or would you prefer it on a plate?'

'Rolls will do fine,' he replied evenly. 'What's upset you, Miss King? You seem – distraught!'

Nicola fumed. 'Don't be ridiculous,' she said tightly. She added ham and lettuce to a roll. 'Mayonnaise?'

'Fine, thank you.'

Nicola supplied him with the roll and extracted a can of beer. 'Where are the glasses?'

'In the hamper at the bottom, but this will do fine for me,' he answered, taking the can from her and peeling back its lid. He raised it to his lips and drank deeply. 'Hmmn, that's good! Warm, but good!'

Nicola busied herself filling another roll. She no longer felt hungry and she knew it would be force-work endeavouring to swallow food. However, after supplying Jason with two more rolls she picked up a banana and began to peel it, hoping the fruit would not stick in her throat.

Jason propped his back against a palm and ate with obvious enjoyment. Nicola moved restlessly, brushing away flies unnecessarily, tidying the hamper, doing anything to distract attention from herself. As each minute passed she became convinced that he knew who she was and was deliberately playing on her nerves with this silence. But even so, if he did know who she was, what of it? She was an employee of Inter-Anglia just as he was and she had a job to do. Why should he imagine she had ulterior motives for coming out here? So why had she denied that Louise was her sister?

Coming to a decision, she said: 'If you must know, Louise Ellison is my sister.'

Jason did not turn a hair. He continued eating his roll. When she was beginning to think he hadn't heard her, he suddenly said:

74

'So why should you deny knowing her?'

Nicola bit her lip. 'Well, I knew that you and she were once – well, acquainted, and I didn't want to embarrass you.' She flushed.

He frowned. 'And you knew I was to be here, didn't you?'

Nicola hesitated. 'Yes,' she said at last. 'Naturally. Sir Harold told me. I had to be briefed about my new boss.'

Jason finished the can of beer, and she passed him another which he opened before speaking again. Then he lay back against the palm and surveyed her lazily. 'I'm surprised you wanted to come out here,' he remarked laconically. 'I should have thought you would have hated my guts!'

Nicola's head jerked up. 'W – Why?'

'Didn't Louise tell you?'

Jason's eyes were very penetrating despite their shielding veil of thick black lashes. Nicola wondered what thoughts were going through his mind. It was a nerve-racking situation.

'Tell me what?' she asked now.

Jason frowned. 'Oh, come on! Louise wasn't the type to keep things to herself.'

Nicola's finger nails bit into the palms of her hands. 'Louise's affairs are no concern of mine,' she denied uncomfortably. 'She's a married woman – and older than I am.'

Jason's eyes narrowed. 'Married – yes,' he said slowly. 'I know.'

Nicola stared at him. 'Didn't that deter you?' The

words were out before she could prevent them.

Jason shrugged. 'I'm not married,' he replied point-edly.

Nicola stifled a retort, opening a can of lager with trembling fingers and pouring some into a glass. Sipping it, she felt a little better. His dispassionate dismissal of Louise's marriage aroused all the hatred she felt towards him. How dared he act so indifferently? He deserved to suffer for what he had done. Somehow she must destroy that insensitive façade, that mocking expression from his handsome face. But could she?

After they had finished the meal, and Jason had started his third can of beer Nicola closed the hamper and settled down on the rug to relax. Jason seemed absorbed in his own thoughts, and Nicola wondered if he would sleep. If he did it would give her a chance to do a little detective work, look through his belongings, perhaps. She didn't know what she expected to find. It would be too much to hope for that she might find something, some evidence, to discredit him in Sir Harold Mannering's eyes. His life was too tidily mapped out, categorized as she had said. His record in that file in London showed how reliable, how methodical in business matters he could be. And when his practical work began to bore him there was always that seat on the board waiting for his acceptance. So neat – so logical, but so cold.

She glanced across at him. Why did he think she had come out here really? He didn't believe she was merely a secretary, and certainly he didn't imagine she was anything to Paul Mannering, so what possible solution had he come up with? Unless he had not come up with any solution, and was merely biding his time, waiting for her to show her hand. Whatever she decided to do it must be done surreptitiously. He must not suspect her real motives. She frowned. It would have been so much easier if he had been a man like Graham Wilson, and after all, she had had no reason to suspect he was not a man like that. A man who pursued married women without thought for their married state ought to have been an easy conquest. But instead all she had succeeded in arousing in him was anger.

She thought about Louise. Poor Louise! She would not have stood a chance against a man like Jason Wilde, who if he chose to exert his concentrated charm and personality could be an overwhelming temptation to someone whose life was dull by comparison. And George, Louise's husband, had long passed the stage of trying to charm his wife. Maybe Louise had not been blameless, but without encouragement she would not have behaved so foolishly.

The heat pressed down on Nicola's eyeballs, and she thought she would just close her eyes for a moment. It was so pleasant lying there. The sound of the water as some insect skimmed its surface was soothing, and there was nothing to disturb the stillness. They might have been alone in the world, the blank expanses of desert stretching away endlessly into the distance.

But when she opened her eyes again, a film of heat had enveloped her body, and she realized with a sense of annoyance that she had been asleep. She sat up abruptly, wondering where Jason Wilde was. Then she relaxed. He was lying on the other side of the hamper, stretched out lazily, his eyes shaded by one arm, while the other rested by his side. She leaned over and read the time. It was already after three o'clock. She must have slept over an hour. She sighed, looking down at him exasperatedly. She had no real idea whether he was carrying a wallet with him or not, and if he was it would most likely be in his back hip pocket, and completely inaccessible.

Quietly she got to her feet, trying not to disturb him. Then she walked to the water's edge and wet her handkerchief again, giving herself a cooling wash. Afterwards she straightened, and glanced across at the Land-Rover. She didn't know why, but something urged her to take a look inside. Crossing the clearing, she slid into her seat, scanning the parcel shelf for any likely item of interest. Jason's papers were there, but a glance at them confirmed that they contained purely technical information relating to the oil rig and pipeline. There was a map of the desert, with information noted upon it of various geological strata, and a kind of gauge which meant nothing to her.

She rifled through the rest of the paraphernalia lying there; empty cigarette cartons, matchboxes, a couple of old newspapers, some sunglasses, rolled-up scraps of paper, a broken pencil. The usual mess of rubbish collected in a car over a period of time. Nothing of any interest to her.

But suddenly her fingers encountered a metal container. It was newer than the rest of the things and from the feel of it far from empty. There was nothing on the outside to indicate what its contents might be and with trembling fingers she prised off the lid. She felt no shame at searching his belongings like this. He was the one who had started it all.

Inside the tin a fine white powder confronted her. It was weighty too, considering the tin was barely half full. She frowned, and bending her head sniffed it cautiously. There seemed to be no smell except one of dryness from the lining of the tin. Her mind darted agilely over the possibilities. Could she have innocently discovered something far more dangerous for him than a mere error in his work? Despite her hatred of him she had thought that in business at least he was an honest man. But what could this substance be that he was concealing so carelessly in the Land-Rover? And yet was it careless? Didn't the very essence of subtlety lie in using ordinary things to their best advantage? If this was what she thought it might be hadn't he chosen quite a clever hiding place? Who would imagine anyone would conceal a quantity of heroin amongst a pile of rubbish on a parcel shelf?

She dipped her finger into the tin and brought out a little to put on her tongue. She tasted it, allowing it to dissolve slowly. It certainly didn't seem familiar, and her pulses raced madly. If Jason Wilde dealt in drugs that might account for him choosing a job here, in the Middle East. Her heart plunged. She must think carefully. What could she do about it?

'Got indigestion?' queried a voice close to her ear, and she almost dropped the tin at the sudden sound of those familiar sardonic tones. Her face suffused with

79

colour and she just stared speechlessly at him for an awful moment.

'Wh – what did you say?' she asked at last, fumblingly replacing the lid of the tin.

Jason straightened from his lounging position outside the vehicle and slid in beside her, forcing her to move across the seats to get away from him.

'I said have you got indigestion?' he repeated quietly.

Nicola swallowed hard, replaced the tin on the shelf, and shook her head. 'No. Why?'

Jason studied her thoughtfully for a minute. 'What did you imagine was in that tin?' he asked flatly.

Nicola lifted her shoulders uncomfortably, finding it difficult to regain her composure. 'I – I didn't think,' she denied awkwardly.

'Didn't you?' Jason was sceptical. 'I think you did. I think you imagined it was some kind of narcotic. That was why you jumped so guiltily when I appeared.'

Nicola didn't reply and Jason lifted the tin into his hands, prising off the lid. He took her hand firmly in one of his and poured a quantity of the powder into her palm. 'Taste it again,' he said quietly. 'Go on.'

'I'd rather not.' Nicola endeavoured to sound indifferent.

'Oh, but I insist,' he commanded softly, and with ill grace Nicola obediently put her hand to her mouth, allowing her tongue to scoop up some of the powder. She got more than she had expected and it effervesced horribly on her tongue, causing her to cough and splutter.

'Ugh!' she gasped, brushing the rest of the powder

on her palm out of the window. 'It's vile!'

'What is it?' asked Jason patiently.

'Bicarbonate of soda,' she said, rubbing her mouth violently with the back of her hand. 'That was a horrible thing to make me do!'

Jason gave her a wry glance. 'You think so? And what were your suspicions? They were pretty horrible, too, weren't they?'

Nicola bent her head. 'Anyway, why keep bicarbonate of soda in the Land-Rover?' she asked angrily, trying to cover herself.

Jason shrugged. 'It belongs to your friend Mannering. His stomach isn't as strong as he thought it was.'

Nicola compressed her lips. She had behaved very foolishly and he had every right to be angry with her. In future she must take care not to jump to such crazy conclusions. But Jason wasn't finished with her yet.

'Tell me,' he said, 'just why were you poking about in here when you thought I was asleep? What were you looking for? Something like you thought you had found?'

'Heavens, no!' Nicola would have slid out of the Land-Rover to get away from his uncomfortably penetrating gaze, but he caught her wrist.

'What, then?'

She fumed. 'Oh, nothing, nothing! Do you mean to say you weren't asleep at all?'

'You woke me, clambering about,' he replied evenly. 'Come on, you might as well spill it. What did Mannering send you out here to accomplish? Does he suspect I'm mixed up in something like narcotics?'

Now Nicola was really in trouble. 'Oh, don't be so ridiculous,' she cried, struggling to free herself. 'You're Sir Harold's blue-eyed boy!'

Jason frowned. 'That description pleases me even less than the last one,' he muttered. 'I don't figure you, Miss King, I don't figure you at all! Okay, I'll accept that you persuaded Mannering to let you come out here with Paul, that wouldn't be too difficult to achieve from the way he regards you. What I don't get is why you should come out here! What's in this for you?' A strange look came over his face. 'Unless – unless you're involved in the same business as I assumed you were accusing me of!'

Nicola's eyes were horrified. 'How can you even think such a thing?'

'You did,' he reminded her. 'Of me!'

Nicola wrenched her arm free. 'If you're read·· I'd like to go back to camp,' she said coldly.

Jason continued to regard her. 'I bet you would,' he muttered. 'Okay, Miss King, now we know where we stand.'

'What do you mean?'

'I know that one way or another you're gunning for me. Well okay, two can play at that game. Just watch your step, Miss King. Or you may find the ground has been cut out from under you.'

Nicola slid out of the vehicle. She was breathing swiftly and she felt a tenseness over all her body. She had made a complete hash of everything now. However would she be able to get close to him when he obviously despised her? And it was all her own fault. If she had only not attempted that amateur effort at detection, none of this would have happened. After all, it had been ridiculous. She had merely succeeded in making a fool of herself. She would have to use much more subtle methods if she was going to attract the attention of a man who was apparently bored with the obvious wiles of the opposite sex.

The drive back to camp was accomplished in silence and when he stopped outside her bungalow she couldn't wait to get out and run indoors. She heard the Land-Rover drive away as she entered the living room and breathed a heavy sigh of relief. On the living room table a letter awaited her. Apparently the post had been collected from Gitana and delivered in her absence. She recognized Louise's handwriting, and flopped down into an easy-chair to read it. She slit open the envelope and took out the note. It was little more, with vaguely derisory allegations towards George who had apparently been to see her. Nicola wondered why, but read on. The rest was concerned with Jason, asking how Nicola was getting on, and hoping she was successful in destroying him as he had destroyed them. She scarcely mentioned the children, and Nicola flung it to one side, not really in the mood for Louise's recriminations.

She went into the bathroom and took a shower before dressing in clean trousers and a more feminine blouse. She would have liked to have worn a skirt, just occasionally, but as she had to go to the canteen for a

83

meal, she knew she mustn't. Then she lit a cigarette and reviewed the events of the day.

Why did she persistently allow Jason Wilde to get her back up? Instead of behaving like a tigress every time she tangled with him, she should allow him the advantage sometimes. A woman's strength lay in weakness, and no man was completely immune to that, were they?

Or was that merely wishful thinking?

He was certainly like no man she had ever encountered before. In her experience men were reasonably uncomplicated beings, whose actions could be channelled by the cunning of their feline counterpart. To encounter a man who seemed capable of gauging her thoughts almost before she was aware of formulating them herself was unnerving, particularly as she suspected his expertise was the result of cold logical reasoning rather than any kind of foreknowledge of her affairs.

The next morning after breakfast, she was on her way to the offices when there was a sudden thundering of hooves across the desert, and even as she stood on the steps of the building a cloud of dust heralded the arrival of a party of Arabs on horseback. They erupted into the camp looking picturesque and exotic in their flowing burnouses, their swarthy features darkened still further by the addition of beards and moustaches. They presented quite a startling spectacle to Nicola and she stood transfixed, watching them as they reared their mounts and wheeled about before halting in front of the office building.

One of the Arabs hastily climbed down and ran to hold the horse of another who dismounted more ceremoniously. His horse was elaborately saddled with jewelled reins and tasselled trappings. He was rather magnificent, too, thought Nicola admiringly, with his glowing dark eyes and thin, aristocratic features. Rings sparkled on every finger, and a heavy beaten gold medallion hung round his neck. His robes were richly embroidered and his sandals were of plaited leather.

If she was studying him, he was certainly studying her, and as she became aware of his scrutiny a wave of hot colour spread up her throat. With an uneasy feeling of having lingered too long she swiftly turned to go, but his voice halted her.

'*Mademoiselle!* Please, a moment.'

Reluctantly she turned, and saw that he was smiling, revealing teeth vividly white in his dusky face. 'Yes?' she said, awkwardly, wondering what Jason Wilde would think if he came upon them now.

The Arab swept her a bow. 'Forgive me, *mademoiselle*, if my foolish eyes betrayed my amazement, but what is a beautiful English rose doing here in our arid desert?'

Nicola swallowed hard. She didn't quite know how to answer that. Fortunately, she was saved the necessity of having to do so, as familiar tones broke the silence that had fallen.

'So, Mohammed! To what do we owe the honour of this visit?'

The Arab turned and Nicola's palms moistened uncomfortably. She was soon to find out what Jason

Wilde thought.

'Ah, Wilde!' The Arab's tones were smooth and honey-soft. 'You did not tell me you had a new and quite unexpected member of your team!'

Jason Wilde surveyed Nicola's flushed face rather sardonically. 'Perhaps that was because the last time I spoke to you I did not know myself,' he replied, equally smoothly. 'Miss King was as you said – an unexpected surprise!'

The tall Arab smiled embracingly. 'So! But not an unpleasant surprise, eh, Wilde? She is – perhaps – a friend of yours?'

Nicola stiffened as Jason gave a sharp denial. He was so cold, so unfeeling. He didn't care what this other man thought so long as he was not personally involved.

'I repeat, Mohammed, what brings you here?' Jason was getting impatient now.

But the Arab was unalarmed. 'Do not disturb yourself, Monsieur Wilde. Naturally I desire an introduction to your – er – assistant.'

Jason thrust his hands deep into the pockets of his cotton trousers. 'Very well,' he agreed chillingly. 'The Sheikh Abi Ben Abdul Mohammed – Miss Nicola King!'

'Enchanted, *mademoiselle*!' The Sheikh saluted her by touching his chest, lips and forehead with his fingers, and then taking her hand he raised it almost to his lips. 'And may I ask how you are liking our country?'

Nicola glanced at Jason, noticing his cold expression. 'I – I like it very much,' she replied truthfully. 'I didn't realize the desert could have such beauty.'

The Sheikh looked pleased. 'Is that so? Then I am delighted. Even though I am sure the desert could never equal your own beauty, Mademoiselle King.'

Nicola linked her fingers together rather awkwardly. She was wholly unused to such florid compliments and didn't quite know how to answer them. So she merely smiled, and began to wish the Sheikh would state his business and go.

Jason studied her expressive face emotionlessly, and then said, with perspicacity: 'I have the feeling you knew Miss King was here before you arrived, Mohammed.'

The Sheikh turned to the tall Englishman with an urbane smile. 'Ah, Wilde, you are astute! Am I so transparent? Yes, of course, I knew. My friend Mustafa was at pains to inform me.'

Jason's brows drew together. 'Mustafa? I might have known.' Then he lifted his shoulders. 'But I understood you and Mustafa were having what you might call a little disagreement.'

Sheikh Abi Ben Abdul Mohammed looked rather amused. 'We were. We were, Wilde. But our differences have now been settled. And after all, why should you be allowed to keep such an advent to our lives such a secret?'

Jason gave Nicola a killing glance, and she shrank back against the support of the building. 'It's no secret, Mohammed,' he snapped. 'As you can see, Miss King is here to work, and for no other reason.'

The Sheikh looked sceptical. 'Nevertheless, one cannot work all the time, Wilde. We should like you to bring Miss King to dine with us.'

Jason shook his head bleakly. 'I am afraid Miss King is much too tired at the end of the day to want to go visiting, Mohammed. I'm sorry.'

Nicola's relief at Jason's command of the conversation evaporated in the heat of the anger he aroused in her at the way he so carelessly dismissed her opinion. He might at least have had the decency to ask her. In consequence, she spoke hastily, and without much forethought.

'On the contrary,' she contradicted him. 'I should love to dine with the Sheikh. I'm not *always* tired, Mr. Wilde. In fact I'm getting quite used to the climate.'

The bombshell exploded, she was immediately contrite, and was overwhelmed by apprehension. What if Jason took her at her word as he had done before and agreed to her dining with the Sheikh – but *alone*! Then she would really be in trouble, for even she realized the dangers in that. Swallowing hard, she dared hardly look at Jason, and her cheeks burned as the Sheikh said: 'You see, Monsieur Wilde, sometimes even you can be mistaken. It is natural that you should feel responsibility for the *mademoiselle*, but as you can see she is more than capable of speaking for herself.'

'I would agree with you there,' remarked Jason, his tones icily polite. He looked at Nicola's bent head, and the penetration of his gaze caused her to glance up at him uneasily. 'Well, of course, if Miss King feels the need for more social contact I will not stand in her way.'

Nicola's heart plunged. 'But — but naturally the Sheikh's invitation is — is for us both,' she stammered, even while anger at his actions simmered inside her.

Jason's eyes were challenging. 'My time is not my own,' he replied suavely. 'I have work to do in the evenings which precludes—'

'Nonsense!' Nicola burst out, before she could prevent herself. 'That is — you — you know very well I couldn't possibly — go — go alone.' Her breast heaved with suppressed emotion, and she felt an immense urge to slap his mocking face.

Then, as though relenting, Jason smiled, but it was not a pleasant smile. He turned to the Sheikh. 'Is Miss King correct? Does your invitation include us both?'

The Sheikh made an expressive gesture. 'But of course. Consider my house honoured to welcome you. As Miss King says, she does require an escort.'

Jason nodded. 'All right.'

'Good. Then I shall expect you both — let me see — would tomorrow evening be too soon?'

Jason shook his head, and Nicola did likewise, and the Sheikh nodded briskly and turned to his retinue. The Arab who had assisted him to dismount rushed forward to help him into his ornate saddle, and with another of those sweeping salutations they wheeled their horses and were gone.

In the ensuing dust-storm they created, Nicola turned away to mount the steps to the office door, but Jason moved more swiftly and was there before her, preventing her entrance. Nicola looked at him, more than ever aware of him as a man, and the awareness brought with it a weakness which assailed her body unwillingly, destroying the defences she might raise against him.

'Oh, please,' she said. 'Not another argument. I know – I know I spoke foolishly, but you deliberately attempted to humiliate me and I couldn't stomach that!'

'I? Humiliate you?' Jason stared at her incredulously. 'My God, I really think you mean that!'

'I do!' Nicola pressed a hand to her throat.

'You have no conception of what you've done, have you? You don't care that you might have jeopardized the success of our development here?'

Nicola gave him an exasperated look. 'I think you're exaggerating everything out of all proportion,' she exclaimed.

'Do you? Do you really? All right, all right. I'll try and explain. Sheikh Abi Ben Abdul Mohammed is one of those men that you can find in any walk of life – a natural trouble-maker. Our being here in Abrahm is a precarious situation. At any moment the Sheikh could find some stupid, senseless reason for forbidding the company the rights here. Right now his hands are tied. This is a friendly country – friendly towards the West, that is – and Mohammed hasn't the power to change his allegiance even though he might want to. But if he could find something – some small reason why he should forbid us the rights then he would be free to follow whatever course he chose. All this trouble we've been having – these unnecessary delays in the pipeline

– they all add up. They're costing the company plenty, and all the time the Sheikh hopes we'll jack it all in and clear out – giving him a free hand. But we aren't so easily put off, as he's discovered, and gradually we're beginning to make headway, with or without his connivance. And now you come here! Threatening to ruin everything! Hell, Mannering must be off his head! I'm convinced he lives in a dream world! Haven't the board any notion of our problems? Does Mannering imagine all these delays we've been having are justified? Does he really believe Mohammed cares a damn about his people?' He raked a hand through his thick hair. 'Am I making myself clear?'

Nicola had been listening intently. When Jason spoke to her like this – treating her as an individual – she found her antipathy towards him disappeared almost completely. It was difficult to remember just why she had come out here; difficult to ignore the sense of his arguments. She had to force her tone to remain light as she said:

'Even so, my dining with the Sheikh is hardly going to create an international incident.'

Jason gave her a disgusted look. 'I don't think you've understood a word I've been saying!' he muttered savagely. 'But don't come crying to me when you find the Sheikh is not one of your prissy English boy-friends!'

Nicola's eyes mirrored her distress for a moment before she hastily disguised it. 'You love hurting me, don't you, Mr. Wilde?' she muttered, in a muffled voice, brushing past him so that he was forced to stand aside to let her into the building.

But he caught her wrist and looked down at her with eyes that burned brilliantly with his anger. 'You are an irresponsible minx, without the sense you were born with,' he muttered violently. 'My God, you've come out here, secure in the knowledge of Mannering's patronage, imagining that you can say and act as you like and there'll be no comeback. Well, let me tell you this, Miss King, we are all men here, with the usual sensual needs, and as Castanya is many hundreds of miles from London, I should guard your tongue or you may find you have more to worry about than the Sheikh Abi Ben Abdul Mohammed!'

Nicola struggled to free herself. 'You're not really threatening me yourself, are you, Mr. Wilde?' she sneered. 'I thought you had oil in your veins – you work so mechanically!'

Jason's eyes darkened, and a thrill of excitement invaded her body, but as suddenly she was free and Graham Wilson was running lightly up the steps to join them, avid to know the reasons for the Sheikh's visit.

Nicola left them, not waiting to greet Graham, and entered her office on trembling legs. Somehow, she felt sure that had Graham Wilson not broken up their confrontation, something momentous would have happened over which she would have had absolutely no control, and the realization was frightening.

# CHAPTER FIVE

NICOLA did not see Jason again until the evening of the following day. She had wanted to see him to ask what she ought to wear for dining with the Sheikh, but he seemed to be deliberately avoiding her, and she hovered uncertainly between the usual pants and blouse she wore for working in, and a rather becoming dress and trouser suit made of navy Crimplene, trimmed with white braid.

Eventually she decided on the dress and trouser suit. After all, she could hardly go out to dine in the same clothes she wore every day, and besides, if the Sheikh did imagine she was interested in him as Jason Wilde had insinuated it wouldn't particularly matter what she wore; the situation would be just the same. And she was feminine enough to want to look her best after so long in the same drab garb.

She brushed her hair until it shone, and secured it with a wide white band, and only applied the lightest of make-ups. She was aware she was sweating as much from nervousness as from the heat and applied an anti-perspirant liberally. She spent a long time studying her reflection, trying to find anything that Jason Wilde might object to, but apart from his obvious objections to her whole appearance there was no especial thing he might disapprove of.

She was pacing about the verandah impatiently at

six-thirty when the Land-Rover drew up, and Jason got out. Tonight, for the first time in their relationship, he was wearing a dark suit and a white shirt, and the formal clothes combined with his tan were quite startlingly attractive. Her stomach gave an uneasy plunge, and she began to wonder whether she had taken too much upon herself by imagining she could challenge a man like him.

He studied her for a moment in the light that was shed filteringly from the room behind her, and then said: 'Are you ready?' in a cool, indifferent voice.

Nicola compressed her lips for a moment, and then she said: 'Yes, I'm ready. Do you – do you think this is all right?' She indicated the navy suit.

Jason's expression was slightly derisive. 'I imagine so. At least I can't accuse you of being scantily dressed.'

Nicola flushed at the mockery in his voice, and then switched off the lights and descended the steps to his side. He opened the Land-Rover's door and she climbed inside wishing desperately that she had not agreed to this outing.

In the blackness of evening, with only a faint moon rising, the desert was wild and desolate, and Nicola felt a sense of relief that Jason should be her escort. He always seemed so dependable somehow, at least in matters of this sort. Emotionally he was enigmatic.

'Is it far?' she ventured when they had left the camp far behind and were climbing some kind of pass through hills which fringed the camp on this side.

Jason shrugged. 'In miles – no; in time, about three-quarters of an hour.'

Nicola digested this, and then she said tentatively, 'I – I – I'd like to apologize – for – for – precipitating this situation.'

Jason gave her a swift glance, his expression hidden in the gloom. 'Indeed,' he remarked uncompromisingly. 'And what am I supposed to say to that? That's all right, Miss King? Don't think any more about it? You're forgiven?'

Nicola sighed exasperatedly. 'Any one of them would do,' she said shortly. 'Honestly, must we spend the whole evening arguing?'

'No. We needn't talk at all. I, at least, have things to think about. I don't need conversation.'

'But I do?'

'You said it, not me.'

Nicola seethed and stared out into the darkness. Was there no getting near to this man? For heaven's sake, Louise had made him out to be a man eager for the company of women, a man who seemingly had no morals, at least so far as married women were concerned. And yet with her, he seemed indifferent. Certainly he had shown no interest in her and their relationship had been stormy to say the least. She thought sinkingly that she might possibly be wise to give up the whole idea and return to England. Sir Harold wouldn't object. He would merely sympathize with her in what he thought had been a lovers' quarrel.

Jason lit a cigarette and drew on it deeply, and Nicola wished he had offered her one. She had not thought to bring her own. But rather than ask she quelled the need that rose in her. However, Jason seemed to sense her restlessness, for he said: 'At the risk of you imagining these are marijuana, would you like a cigarette?'

Nicola grimaced in the darkness and accepted one with ill grace. When it was lit, she turned sideways in her seat and studied his profile outlined against the lighter background of the velvety sky outside. She wondered what he was thinking about, what really stirred him. It was not too difficult to arouse him to awareness of her, but only by angering him. Was there no way she could appeal to him in a different manner?

Jason glanced sideways at her. 'Well?' he said. 'What are you thinking now?'

Nicola ran her tongue over her lower lip. 'I was thinking about you,' she replied provocatively.

'Oh, yes?' His voice had hardened considerably.

'Yes. What makes you tick, Mr. Wilde? What goes on inside that cold brain of yours?'

'In what way, Miss King?'

Nicola shrugged. 'Have you ever been in love, Mr. Wilde?' It was a daring question and one which she did not expect an answer to.

But Jason merely raised his shoulders in an expressive gesture, and said: 'That's a rather old-fashioned idea, isn't it, Miss King? I thought your generation had thrown that sort of thing out of the window. I mean – being in love implies a permanent relationship. I thought that kind of union was out of date.'

Nicola controlled her temper with difficulty. 'You talk about my generation as though it was different from yours,' she said coolly. 'Besides, I'm an old-fashioned girl. At least in so far as marriage is concerned.'

'You surprise me. I should have thought a – well, satisfying relationship was far more important to a girl like yourself.'

Nicola pressed out the cigarette although it was only half-smoked. 'You are the most despicable man I've ever had the misfortune to meet,' she muttered angrily. 'I can't imagine how Louise—' She broke off abruptly, and clenched her fists. Steady, she told herself chidingly. Don't say any more!

'You can't imagine how Louise – what?' He looked across at her, his expression hidden. 'Made a fool of herself, perhaps?'

Nicola counted to ten. 'I rather think you were the one who made a fool of my sister, Mr. Wilde,' she said tersely.

'Well, you think what you like, Miss King,' he said curtly, 'but believe me, your sister is not the sainted creature you seem to think her!'

Nicola glared at him. 'You're in no position to judge anyone!' she countered angrily.

'I'm not judging, Miss King! You're the one who's attempting to do that. I'm stating facts.'

'As you see them!'

'Well, I could hardly state them as someone else saw them, now could I?' he questioned more mildly, and Nicola shifted in her seat so that she was looking out of the window again. 'Tell me,' he continued, 'if you felt so strongly about your sister, why did you come out here, knowing you were to be working with me?'

Nicola decided it was time to cool the conversation. 'I didn't actually say that,' she replied slowly. 'You practically called my sister a fool. I could hardly ignore that.'

'All right, all right. Leave it.' He was beginning to sound bored.

Nicola moved restlessly in her seat. This was no good, no good at all. Her attempts at getting him to talk more personally about himself only seemed to result in disagreements of one sort or another, and while they were disagreeing she was getting nowhere with him. Why couldn't he have just been the sort of man who reacted favourably towards feminine provocation?

The headlights picked out the rocky terrain they were crossing, a barren area where scrub grass struggled for survival. The Land-Rover bumped and rocked alarmingly at times, and for a while Nicola became absorbed in her surroundings. Once she saw the glimmer of water in the headlights and glanced questioningly at Jason. Obligingly, he said:

'That was a *guelta* – a rock pool. They spring up here and there – a necessary adjunct in terrain as bare as this. Early in the morning, and at nightfall, it's the meeting place for the desert people. They bring their herds to water. Sometimes they bathe – wash clothes. The normal chores that women perform the world over.'

'I'd like to come here in daylight,' said Nicola. 'Is it beautiful?'

'I suppose there is beauty in everything if you look for it,' he replied quietly. 'To me the desert is beautiful – not in the way that England or Jamaica or even the Pacific is beautiful. They rely on water to add to their natural landscaping. Here the colours are brilliantly defined. The air is crystal clear – lucid!' He sighed. 'One can see for miles from the heights of these passes, over sand and rock and palm – to infinity.'

Nicola frowned. 'I'm surprised you feel like that when you are in a way responsible for destroying the natural landscape,' she said. 'I mean – the oil fields are not pretty sights, are they?'

'Oh, no.' Jason nodded. 'But without oil, these people will never achieve any kind of life for themselves. The nomads may not want the kind of life we would call civilized, but they should have the choice, the right to choose for themselves. Right now, these people are living in the way they have lived for hundreds of years.'

'And oil makes a country rich?'

'Financially, yes. They need schools, hospitals, social services! The wealth will pay for these things. Out here, children die from diseases they can neither diagnose nor treat. Simple things that our children would never succumb to. And there's always the heat, and the dirt, and the flies. Killers in themselves.'

Nicola nodded herself. 'And this Sheikh – this man we're going to dine with – he holds the balance of power?'

'At the moment. It's a precarious position at best. Any one of a dozen uprisings could overthrow him.

That's why he wants to make his position secure before such an eventuality occurs.'

'And Mustafa – the other Arab we went to see – where does he come in?'

'He doesn't. At least, he hasn't much influence. You may recall I said that he and Mohammed had had a difference of opinion. Well, obviously, somehow the breach has been healed. It could be in one of a dozen ways. Mustafa is unpredictable – sometimes adversary, sometimes friend. If Mohammed has won his confidence then possibly he has supplied him with arms – who can say? It's a complex business – and one which, thankfully, we don't become involved in. So far as Inter-Anglia are concerned it doesn't particularly matter who is in power, so long as we are allowed to continue drilling.'

They had descended to the plain now and soon they were approaching what appeared to be a small township. In the darkness, it had a romantic air, but Jason soon dispelled any romanticism that Nicola might be feeling.

'This is Abyrra,' he remarked laconically. 'We don't go into the town. The Sheikh's residence is happily on this side. It's as well for your sake. The poverty and squalor we might find would appal you.'

'What do you mean?'

'I mean that the majority of the civilian population live in crumbling dwellings that provide no sanitation of any kind. Apart from a few huts, these buildings, and some haphazard shops there's a kind of central square that serves as a kind of meeting place, and that is Abyrra.'

Nicola sighed. 'Looking ahead – the white-painted buildings look rather attractive,' she said.

'Yes. But in daylight you would see that the white paint is flaking and daubed with mud and filth. Children have long since destroyed any remnants of past civilizations which might have been of interest to the archaeologist.'

'You certainly don't intend that I should find anything attractive here,' she said impatiently. 'Heavens, it can't be that bad!'

Jason refrained from answering, and Nicola had the feeling that he didn't much care what she thought. He had been stating facts, and whether or not she chose to accept them was of complete indifference to him.

They had turned up a rocky sweep towards a fortified dwelling on the outskirts of the community. Tall gates guarded an inner courtyard, where several uniformed guards were patrolling. Certainly there was nothing slipshod about the way they thoroughly examined the occupants of the vehicle, and then saluted when they recognized Jason. Another guard conducted them inside, leading the way along a corridor lit at intervals by huge burnished lamps. There was a faint smell of something like incense, and the coolness of the night air could not be appreciated in such a humid atmosphere. But at least the aromas here were not unpleasant, and Nicola looked about her with great interest. Here there was evidence of great wealth of a kind she had never before experienced.

They were conducted to a huge chamber ornately

decorated with silken hanging tapestries, the floor strewn with skin rugs and soft cushions. There was a carpet of an oriental design into which Nicola's feet sank, and reclining on a kind of dais before a low table absolutely groaning under the weight of the food upon it was the Sheikh Abi Ben Abdul Mohammed. He was dressed tonight in a rich silken robe, edged with scarlet thread, while several necklaces of gold and jewels adorned his neck. Rings sparkled on every finger as before, but Nicola was sure they were not the same rings as she had seen the previous day.

He rose adroitly at their entrance, and came to greet them, his eyes surveying Nicola thoroughly, taking in every detail of her charming appearance. The penetration of that look caused Nicola to feel that every inch of her body had turned a brilliant shade of tomato, and she had the feeling he was mentally taking her apart, examining every limb, every muscle, with an educated eye. As though she were a contender for his harem, Nicola thought incredulously, and felt the first twinges of alarm slide along her spine. She glanced at Jason and found his eyes upon her too, a strange gleam in their depths, and immediately felt slightly reassured. She stepped a little closer to him, and when the Sheikh took her hand to draw her to his table she felt an awful sense of reluctance to leave Jason's side.

But after all, it was not so bad. They were joined at dinner by the Sheikh's eldest son, a young man who was introduced as Victor. He was about eighteen, Nicola thought, and the Sheikh proudly explained that he was to go to Oxford the next year to complete his education. Unlike the Sheikh, Victor wore European clothes and seemed eager to learn as much as he could about the European way of life. He knew the names of some of the popular artists of the day, and Nicola could talk quite naturally to him, finding relief in his uncomplicated conversation.

The meal was long and varied. Some of the courses she could not even put a name to, but she recognized a *pilaff* of goat's meat, and *chorba*, which is a sort of macaroni stew, and which she had already tasted back at the camp. There was cheese, and fish, nuts and dates, dishes of fruit preserved in syrup which was delicious, and aromatic continental coffee.

Afterwards, when the servants had cleared all but the fruit and dates from the table, the Sheikh summoned a troupe of dancers who, together with three musicians, performed a rather unrhythmic shuffle around the centre of the floor. The music, strange and unmelodic, did not appeal to Nicola, and she was quite willing to lounge on her cushions and listen when the Sheikh spoke to her.

'Tell me,' he said softly, 'what do you think of my humble abode?'

Nicola glanced at him, and then shrugged. 'I am sure you are aware that your abode is anything but humble,' she replied easily. 'And I must admit I think the decorations are quite exotic.'

'Hmm.' The Sheikh drew on the cigar he was smoking. 'Do you like Abrahm, Miss King?'

'Quite well,' she answered. 'I've never been to Africa before.'

'But this is North Africa – and quite different from Central and Southern Africa, you will find,' said the Sheikh smoothly. 'Here, our civilization can be traced back thousands of years.'

Nicola nodded. 'I should imagine this whole area provides historical interest for museums and archaeological institutes the world over,' she agreed. 'Nowadays people are beginning to realize that only from the past can we learn about the future.'

The Sheikh looked pleased. 'That is indeed an astute observation from one so young, Miss King,' he said, studying her more intently. 'There are so many people who believe our future lies in the stars – in the outer limits of endless space. This I cannot accept. Here, within our own sphere, lie all the answers to the mysteries of life. It is all written, and there is no escape from destiny, fate, what have you.'

'You're a fatalist, Sheikh Mohammed.'

'But of course. Still – enough of the past, let us concentrate on the present. It is not every day my house is honoured by the visit of such charming company.'

Nicola smiled. The wine she had drunk with the meal and afterwards had relaxed her somewhat and she felt less embarrassed by his flattery. 'You're very kind,' she said.

'Kind? No. Truthful, *mademoiselle*, that is all. It is so delightful to see a fair complexion after so many dark ones. Tell me, from whom did you inherit this honey-gold hair?'

Nicola's cheeks coloured. 'From – from my mother, I suppose,' she replied awkwardly. 'She was much fairer than I.'

'Blonder, perhaps, fairer – no!' The Sheikh's dark eyes were intent. 'I find you quite enchanting, *mademoiselle*. You must come here again. I desire your company.'

Nicola didn't quite know whether she liked that word 'desire'. It implied a more intimate relationship, and one which she did not wish to foster. She must be careful. Her brain was clear enough to register this.

'A moment,' said the Sheikh, now, as she would have turned to Jason to say something – *anything*! He thrust his hand into the folds of his robe and withdrew a small box which he placed firmly in her hand. 'Open it,' he commanded gently. 'I insist.' And Nicola felt sure he would have done so had she not immediately complied.

Inside, on a bed of white satin, lay a pendant on a slender gold chain. It was an emerald, iridescent and magnificent, and the size of a huge teardrop.

'Oh,' she said, in astonishment. 'Oh, it's beautiful!'

'You like it?' The Sheikh's eyes probed hers.

'Well – well, of course. Anyone would.' Nicola bit her lip.

'It is the colour of your eyes, *mademoiselle*. Emerald – purest emerald. Take it. It's yours!'

Nicola felt as though she was gaping at him, and controlled herself instantly, but the thought that he might offer her a present like this had not occurred to her. She thrust it back into his hand. 'No,' she gasped firmly. 'No, really, I appreciate the compliment you've paid me – but no, I couldn't possibly accept such a gift.'

The Sheikh refused to accept the box, however, and she sat there feeling lost and unable to express her position. She looked desperately at Jason, and succeeded in drawing his attention to herself. She looked expressively at the jewel case, but he merely lifted his shoulders ever so slightly, as much as to say 'I told you so'.

She began to panic, stammering excuses out uncomfortably, that in England a girl did not accept expensive gifts of this kind, that it would not be right, that he would place her in a dreadful position. The Sheikh listened calmly, a strange expression playing round his finely chiselled lips, an expression which made Nicola wonder whether he had planned all this just to embarrass her. If so, then Jason was doing absolutely nothing to extricate her, and the anger against herself that she was feeling increased to encompass him too. She began to blame him for the whole thing, and silently and bitterly berated him. Finally, when she was running out of anything to say, Jason intervened.

'What Miss King is trying not very successfully to explain is that the acceptance of such a gift could be misconstrued, Mohammed,' he said. 'Now, we are men of the world, and I am sure your reasons for offering such a gift were entirely without motive, but there are others who might place an entirely different construction on such a situation.'

The Sheikh's eyes narrowed. 'What misconstruction could be placed upon my offering a gift to a young woman who I admire immensely?' he murmured. 'I was not aware that I had to provide you with my motives for doing such a thing, Monsieur Wilde!' A menacing note had crept into his voice now, and Nicola felt a shiver run up her spine.

Jason gave her a cold, quelling glance, and then resumed his conversation with their host. 'You are prepared to say that you have a motive?' he asked bleakly.

The Sheikh moved his head consideringly. 'Miss King appeals to me as no European woman has ever done,' he replied smoothly. 'Is it so inconceivable that she might find me a little appealing also?' He spread his hands. 'After all, did she not express a wish to dine with me here?'

Nicola's eyes were wide and disturbed. Whatever could Jason say to that? She sensed his anger, but was helpless to come to her own aid. Leaning forward, she placed the case containing the pendant on the low table, and then sat back, clasping her hands tightly together. She was aware that Victor was eyeing her strangely now, and she wondered whether he was used to his father discussing the merits of the women with whom he dined.

Jason rose abruptly to his feet. 'I am afraid there has been a misunderstanding, Mohammed,' he said slowly. 'Yesterday, when you encountered — Miss King, and myself, it appeared that we were — what shall I say? — antagonists. Of course, this is not so. What you witnessed was in effect — a lovers' quarrel!'

Nicola's eyes were huge and she stared at Jason incredulously.

He went on: 'We have not advertised it – or made it generally known among the men – but Miss King is in fact – my fiancée.' He ignored the sceptical stare of the Sheikh and continued: 'Naturally, the reason Miss King came out here was a legitimate one – that of helping me with my reports and so on. But Sir Harold Mannering is aware of the real relationship between us, is this not so, Nicola?'

Nicola sat up straight. 'Oh – oh, yes, indeed,' she hastened into speech. 'But – but I thought we agreed it was to be – our secret!'

Jason's eyes were glittering angrily, but his lashes veiled them from the Sheikh's piercing gaze. 'I am sure we can trust Sheikh Mohammed,' he said insinuatingly. 'He is an understanding man. And admiring you as he does, I am sure he must – envy me.'

Sheikh Mohammed got to his feet too, standing legs apart, staring at Jason as though endeavouring to force him into admitting he had made the whole story up. Then he turned and stared at Nicola's bent head. She did not trust her own ability to confront his dark eyes. She scrambled to her feet, and Jason glanced pointedly at his watch.

'It is getting late, Sheikh Mohammed,' he said politely. 'I think it is time we took our leave of you. We have a long drive back to Castanya.'

The Sheikh considered him broodingly for a few minutes longer, and then said: 'So be it.' He turned to Nicola, and before she could withdraw raised her hand to his lips. 'I will not say good-bye, Miss King, but merely *au revoir*. I am sure we will meet again.'

Nicola swallowed hard and managed an embarrassed nod, then she moved swiftly to Jason's side. In keeping with their newly acquired position he looked gently down at her and took her hand in one of his. The firm pressure of his fingers on hers was reassuring, although she had the feeling that she had not heard the last of this. She supposed she ought to be delighted at the subterfuge he had adopted. He seemed to have played right into her hands. Why was it then that she felt such a terrible feeling of helplessness?

# CHAPTER SIX

THE night air had never seemed more refreshing or invigorating, and Nicola breathed deeply as they climbed into the Land-Rover, mentally gathering all her small store of defences. She could sense Jason's hostility and there was more than a twinge of apprehension in the glances she cast in his direction. But Jason did not look at her or speak to her, starting the vehicle's engine silently and driving out of the courtyard, swinging smoothly on to the road to Castanya. Soon the crumbling mass that was Abyrra was left far behind, and they were ascending the pass between the mountains that earlier they had descended. The breeze that blew through the open windows was cool and there was not the dust tonight to invade their throats with its choking embrace.

Finally, Nicola broke the silence by saying: 'For heaven's sake, let's get it over with,' in a taut, nervous voice.

Jason barely glanced at her. 'What is there to get over?' he questioned coldly. 'It surely isn't necessary for me to labour the point any further. Tonight, for the first time, I think, you've realized the danger in irresponsible actions.'

'How was I to know the Sheikh would – well, behave as he did?' she asked exasperatedly. 'Heavens, this is the twentieth century!'

'Not out here. The twentieth century barely touches their lives. I explained that to you on our way to Abyrra. Didn't it register at all?'

Nicola sighed. 'Oh, I suppose it did. But not to the extent of including my own position. Besides, I have the feeling that the Sheikh's behaviour was deliberate. I don't think he really desired my company. I think it was a calculated attempt to create an impossible situation.'

Jason gave a short mirthless laugh. 'Good, I suppose I ought to be thankful for small mercies. At least your common sense asserted itself sufficiently to make you see that Mohammed is not the simple-minded individual he would have you believe. Of course his behaviour was deliberate, of course his desire for your company was tempered by self-interest, and of course he intended to create an impossible situation! But what you don't seem to have gathered is that whether this position was artificially or naturally created, it is equally untenable.'

Nicola digested this. 'Our – our engagement, you mean,' she said at last.

'Yes.'

'But – but I thought he didn't really believe you.'

'I don't suppose he did. Nevertheless, so long as you are in Abrahm, you'll be unable to deny it.'

Nicola compressed her lips thoughtfully. Of course, Jason was right. She was beginning to become aware of the precariousness of their position in Abrahm with Sheikh Abi Ben Abdul Mohammed in command, and it would not do to attempt to fool him. And if their 'engagement' should suddenly terminate, he might choose to intimidate the company still further. What she ought to do was take the next plane back to London, and thus avoid this terrible uncertainty, but if she did her chance of getting even with Jason Wilde would terminate too. She would never again have such an ideal opportunity, and surely this whole situation should be to her advantage. By adopting her as his fiancée he had given her a wonderful chance of humiliating him. After all, once the men on the camp knew of their assumed relationship there would be bound to be talk and speculation, and Jason stood to lose so much more than she did. Of course, if he had had any idea of the real reasons for her coming to Castanya he would never have granted her his patronage. But he didn't know and now, instead of feeling sorry for herself, she should be making the most of her advantage. Sir Harold would be delighted at this turn of events. No matter how Jason might phrase it, his chairman would think that Nicola had achieved what she set out to achieve. Besides, he wanted Jason married. He wanted his business intelligence on the board of Inter-Anglia, and so long as Jason remained a bachelor, his chances of settling down remained nebulous.

So with these thoughts in her mind, she said: 'Why should I want to deny it?' in a provocative tone.

Jason stifled an epithet that sprang to his lips, and instead said: 'You won't have time to do so anyway. I intend that you should return to London at the earliest possible opportunity.'

Nicola's eyes widened. This wasn't at all what she wanted.

'You can't make me go back,' she said hotly. 'Sir Harold Mannering sent me out here. He will recall me.'

Jason swung the Land-Rover across a stretch of rocky terrain, and brought it abruptly to a halt beside the gleam of water Nicola had noticed on their way to Abyrra, the *guelta*. Even in the light of the headlights, and the moon that sailed serenely overhead, Nicola could see that it was a strange place. Surrounded by rugged rocks, the water seemed to have a life of its own, and there seemed no possible reason for its conception. Without waiting for more remonstrances which she was sure were to come from Jason, Nicola slid out of the car and walked to the rocks at the water's edge, looking down into seemingly bottomless depths. It would have been nice to swim, but surprisingly the desert night was cold, and she rubbed her elbows with the palms of her hands, warming herself. Her hair had fallen forward hiding her face, and yet she was conscious of Jason's presence beside her and she shivered slightly. Holding back her hair with one hand, she looked up at him, seeing his face clearly in the moonlight.

'Am I such a nuisance to you?' she murmured softly. 'Are you so keen to get rid of me?'

Jason's eyes darkened. 'Don't try anything, Nicola,' he muttered.

The palms of her hands were suddenly moist, and her whole being felt warm. But Jason was still so cold.

'Don't you like me at all, Jason?' she asked appealingly.

Jason's expression was derisive now. 'What is this?' he asked abruptly. 'Are you wanting to compare notes with Louise when you get back?'

Nicola's self-control snapped, and forgetting what he had said that other time she had performed such an action she slapped him hard across his handsome face, standing staring at him in fascinated apprehension as red marks appeared on his cheek. Then, as though realizing what she had done, she turned to run back to the comparative security of the Land-Rover, but Jason caught her upper arms from behind, his grip cruelly bruising her soft flesh so that she cried out in pain, struggling violently. But she knew, without being told, that there was no one to come to her rescue here. Without thought for her clothes he swung her round, pressing her back against a rough, damp outcrop of rock, holding her there helplessly with the weight of his body, while his hands held her face roughly as he bent his head and fastened his mouth to hers.

She had imagined that he might kiss her one day, but in her imaginings it had been a gentle thing, a growing awareness of her that she could use to her own advantage. But there was nothing gentle about him now, and the kisses he was forcing on her parted lips were hard and passionate and demanding, destroying her feeble defences, commanding a response. She pressed her hands against his chest, trying to push him away, but it was an impossible task. Jason was a powerful man, and as he continued to kiss her expertly the

114

desire to escape was rapidly leaving her. She began to weaken, becoming aware of other sensations. She liked the feel of those hard brown hands against her skin, and there was a vague male scent about him of tobacco and shaving cream and warmth.

But something, some inner strength asserted itself, and with a superhuman effort she managed to roll sideways against the rock and free herself. She knew he had let her go, and that she alone had not been responsible for her escape, but that did not prevent her from still feeling shocked and frightened, as much by her own weakness as Jason's expertise.

She glanced back at him, relaxing lazily against the rocks, studying her pale face and tumbled hair. 'Well?' he said mockingly. 'Was it worth the trouble?'

Nicola swallowed hard, incapable at this moment of subterfuge. 'I – I think you're – you're terrible!' she said shakily.

He straightened. 'I'm sorry,' he mocked. 'I'll try to do better next time.'

Nicola gave an involuntary gasp. 'That – that wasn't what I meant, and you know it,' she cried. 'You – you hurt me!'

Jason shrugged his shoulders, and ran a careless hand through his hair, walking indolently towards the Land-Rover. 'That slap you gave me didn't exactly improve my health,' he remarked lazily. 'Come on. I haven't the patience to discuss this any further tonight. Get in the car! I'm tired!'

Nicola did as he asked with ill grace, casting angry glances in his direction to which he seemed completely impervious. She was tired herself, too tired to assimilate what had happened in perspective and to decide what she intended to do next.

The next morning she was awake at an early hour, a feeling of foreboding depriving her of any more rest. Even so, she was loath to leave her bed and considered pretending to be ill to avoid the imminent conflict. But she was not by nature a defeatist, so instead she slid out of bed and went to take her shower. Once dressed in the usual levis and cotton shirt she felt slightly better and more capable of facing whatever was to come.

However when she reached the canteen another surprise awaited her. For some reason she had become the cynosure of all eyes and as she made her way to her table the reason became evident. Lying on the table was a sheaf of cream roses, beautiful things whose perfume scented the atmosphere deliciously. For a heart-stopping moment she thought Jason must have sent them in an attempt to prove his actions of the night before had not been irresponsible, but sanity was instantly restored when she read Sheikh Abi Ben Abdul Mohammed's signature at the end of the message which was written on a white card accompanying the flowers. It read: *To the woman who has succeeded in lighting a fire in the heart of Jason Wilde.*

Nicola glanced round at the groups of men who were watching her, gauging her reactions, and felt embarrassment envelop her. She should have known that Sheikh Abi Ben Abdul Mohammed would not let such an opportunity go to waste. Had Jason seen these flowers? Did he already know about the message?

She swallowed hard, trying to still her racing pulses, when a voice beside her said: 'Sit down, Nicola. It's not the end of the world.'

She swung round to face Paul Mannering. 'Paul!' she exclaimed, something very much like relief in her voice. 'Oh, Paul, have you seen this?'

'Sure. I should think everyone on the camp knows about it by now. Sit down. Sit down. I want to talk to you.'

Nicola subsided weakly into a chair and Paul seated himself opposite her. A pointed glance around the room from him succeeded in stemming some of the speculative glances, and most of the men began to get on with their meal, and talk became general again.

'Heavens above,' said Nicola cupping her face in both her hands, resting her elbows on the table. 'Does Jason know about these?'

'I guess so. But, Nicola, what is all this? I mean – is it true? Are you and Jason – well—' His voice trailed away.

Nicola sighed. She couldn't tell him the truth, but on the other hand she couldn't pretend a situation which he would know was faked. Deciding her best solution was to use the story she had used on his father, she said:

'Well, if I tell you, will you promise to keep it to yourself?'

Paul shrugged. 'I guess so.'

'Well, you see – Jason and I knew one another – back in England about a year ago. I didn't work for

Inter-Anglia then. I worked for an advertising agency, but I got to know Jason and – fell in love with him.'

Paul frowned. 'Go on.'

'Jason was and still is, I suppose, very keen on his work, and I resented it. We quarrelled and he left for another overseas assignment. I knew I needed to see him again – to have a chance to show him I was sorry for what I'd said. When a vacancy was advertised for secretarial work with Inter-Anglia, I applied.' She lifted her shoulders expressively. 'I suppose it sounds silly to you, but I thought if I worked for the same company I might be able to understand everything so much better, as well as providing opportunities for seeing Jason again. But of course, he was moved to this assignment and as the months passed I became convinced he would find someone else – before I had the chance to show I really cared. So as your father, Sir Harold, was a reasonable man I suggested I should be allowed to come out here with you. Your problems came at a very opportune moment for me. Besides, you must know that your father would like to see Jason married and settled in England.'

Paul was looking very sceptical and Nicola wondered whether she had said anything which might betray her real position. After all, Paul knew Jason quite well, and it was possible he had known about Louise. If he should recognize her resemblance to Louise it might present a very awkward situation particularly as he would then know her story had been all fabrication.

At last, he said: 'I know my father wants Jason to

get married. From time to time he has provided suitable applicants for the position of Mrs. Jason Wilde, but Jason wasn't having any.'

Nicola flushed. 'That's why it's so wonderful that he should have chosen me,' she enthused.

Paul pulled a wry face. 'Hmn! It's strange he never showed any emotion when you arrived.'

Nicola managed a light smile. 'Naturally he was shocked, and as he didn't want our relationship publicized what else could he do? As it is, Sheikh Mohammed has done all this without our consent.'

'Has he?' Paul was thoughtful, studying her with an intensity that was rather disturbing. 'You say you knew Jason when he was in England a year ago? As I recall it, the last time Jason was in England he was having trouble with some woman called Louise Ellison.'

Nicola's eyes nearly popped out of her head. 'Who – who did you say?' she asked cautiously.

'Well, it was something like that,' said Paul. 'I know Ellison was her surname. If you and he were so close, how come he was seeing this Ellison woman?'

Nicola shook her head. 'I – I really don't know. Did – did you get to meet this – this other woman?'

'Yeah, I met her. She was once at this club with Jason when I was there myself.' He lit a cigarette thoughtfully. 'I never could understand what he saw in her. She wasn't his type. Flung herself at his head, she did.'

Nicola stiffened. 'How can you make such an observation?' she asked coldly.

Paul snorted derisively. 'Because it turned out she

was married, and I know Jason. I may not like him much, he's too much like Dad, but because of that I know he doesn't run after married women. She must have run after him.'

Nicola bent her head. 'I see,' she said, trying to remain calm.

Paul shrugged. 'Anyway, you're a cool one, coming out here like this uninvited. Didn't it occur to you that Jason might have changed his mind?'

Nicola contained her temper. 'No,' she said shortly. 'That did not occur to me.'

Paul made an indifferent gesture. 'Anyway, you're here now, and you seem to have achieved your objective. When was the relationship clinched?'

'Last night,' remarked a cool, indolent voice from behind Nicola, and they both looked up into Jason Wilde's thin face.

Nicola trembled a little. How long had he been standing there? Paul had been so intent on her conversation it was possible he had been there and not been noticed. However, she managed a smile, and said: 'Have you seen my roses?' in a casual tone.

Jason took the third seat at the table. 'Yes,' he said, nodding. 'I've seen them. They arrived very early. The Sheikh has a special hothouse garden where such blooms flourish. I understand his gardener is French.'

Nicola glanced across at the group of men at the table nearest to theirs. They were eyeing Jason keenly, and she wondered how long this sense of being an oddity would last. She looked at Jason, and then away again when his eyes turned in her direction.

Paul watched their expressions and then got lazily to his feet. 'Far be it from me to act the gooseberry,' he remarked laconically. 'Besides, if I don't hurry I won't have time for breakfast.'

'That's right,' agreed Jason coolly, and with a casual salute Paul walked away.

Nicola bent her head, studying her finger-nails intently, and Jason said: 'As you can see, our "engagement" has caused quite a stir.'

'Yes.' Nicola linked her fingers. 'I've gathered that.'

'And what were you and Paul in such close consultation about? I shouldn't have thought that was the usual behaviour of a girl newly engaged to be married to another man.'

Nicola's head jerked up. 'The men know I came out here with Paul. Surely we're entitled to be friends.'

'Okay, so what were you telling him?'

Nicola compressed her lips. 'If you must know I was telling him that we'd known one another back in England.' She had to say that. If Paul brought up such a thing with Jason he would be bound to be suspicious unless she got her explanation in first.

'You told him *what*?' Jason stared at her incredulously.

Nicola sighed. 'Well, obviously, the idea of us getting to know one another a couple of weeks ago and falling in love doesn't quite fall in with your he-man image, does it?' she exclaimed. 'It was far better for me to pretend that you and I were old acquaintances than to plead an instant attraction.'

Jason studied her carefully. 'All right,' he said slowly, 'I'll buy that. In fact, maybe that's a good idea. For all the men, I mean. I'll think about it. As to the rest, I suppose you're agreed that your best course of action is to return home before Sheikh Abi Ben Abdul Mohammed decides our relationship is less than loving!'

Nicola's eyes widened. 'What do you mean?'

'Hell, I told you last night,' muttered Jason, leaning across the table so that his face was very close to hers.

'You did a lot of things last night,' she hissed back at him.

Jason's tan darkened slightly. 'Don't ride me, Nicola,' he bit out savagely. 'You can't fight me!'

His arrogant words combined with Paul's information of what Jason had implied about her sister were sufficient to infuriate Nicola. 'Can't I?' she asked now in reply to his statement. 'Why not? What can you threaten me with? So far as everyone here is concerned we're engaged to be married, or as good as. The fact that the Sheikh hasn't actually mentioned an engagement in this note doesn't mean he's not going to. He's probably saving that for another occasion. As for Sir Harold Mannering, when he hears the story I should imagine he'll feel delighted that you've finally decided to put an end to your bachelor status!'

Jason's eyes narrowed. 'Just what am I supposed to glean from that?' he asked tautly. 'That you intend informing Sir Harold Mannering that we're engaged?' His tone was derisive.

Nicola traced a pattern on the formica table top with her forefinger. A plan was forming in her mind and she was beginning to realize how she could put it into action. But it was not yet time to become too clever with Jason. He would soon suspect something was up if she became too demanding. Her best plan at the moment was to disarm him, make her position secure, convince him that what she was intending was a reasonable suggestion.

'I've been thinking,' she said slowly. 'You're very keen to send me back to London and discharge your responsibilities, but have you thought what the possible outcome of that action might be?'

'What do you mean?'

'Well, you're always telling me how Sheikh Mohammed is a very suspicious man. Don't you think he'll be exceedingly suspicious if the day after we announce our engagement, our secret engagement, I'm suddenly dispatched back to London like an unwanted package?'

Jason took out his cigarettes and offered her one and when they were both lit he eyed her thoughtfully. 'I never knew you were so concerned about the company's affairs,' he remarked dryly.

Nicola half smiled. 'Don't be sarcastic,' she said easily. 'You know I'm right.' She pressed home the advantage. 'Besides, surely now that we are "engaged", I'm safe enough.'

Jason shook his head. 'I don't know,' he muttered. 'I don't get you — I don't get you at all! I still don't know why you came out here.'

'I've explained all that,' replied Nicola, gathering confidence from his puzzlement. Just for a moment she felt a twinge of something like conscience, and something else; something that had to do with the emotions he had aroused in her the previous evening. A sense of doubt as to her own ability to carry this through without flinching. She couldn't be feeling sorry for him, could she? Not sorry for Jason Wilde! It was impossible! Nevertheless, she knew that in other circumstances the whole affair might well have ended very differently. Perhaps it was just as well she had Louise to keep in mind. Without that she might have found herself wading through a situation fraught with difficulties. Jason was too attractive, too much of a challenge to any woman, and last night he had proved he was no novice when it came to getting what he wanted. She could recall with a kind of painful pleasure the feel of his hands against her soft skin, the hard length of his body pressed against hers, the possessing hunger of his mouth. She felt a trembling awareness of her own vulnerability. This was no easy task she had set herself. She was beginning to realize that.

'Well,' she said now, forcing her thoughts back into less dangerous channels, 'do you see what I am getting at?'

Jason drew on his cigarette, and lay back in his chair surveying her lazily. There was something indolent and mocking about him and even now she wasn't certain she had any advantage at all. 'You want to stay out here, is that right?' he was asking. 'Whatever the consequences?'

Nicola shrugged. 'If you want to put it like that,' she said shortly.

Jason shook his head. 'And what about Harold?'

Nicola swallowed hard. 'I think we should tell him the same story,' she said.

'*What!*' Jason gazed at her disbelievingly. 'You can't seriously expect me to swallow that!'

Nicola moved restlessly. 'Why not? If you tell him the truth he may insist I return to London at once.'

Jason grimaced, 'Good God, if I thought that, do you think I *wouldn't* tell him?'

Nicola heaved a sigh. He was impossible! Just as she seemed to be making headway he ridiculed all her efforts.

'Do you know what I think?' went on Jason coolly. 'I think this whole situation was engineered between you and Mannering. I think your reasons for coming out here were quite simple – to trap me into a situation where I would be practically duty bound to agree to marry you!'

This was too much!

Nicola rose to her feet. 'Don't flatter yourself, Mr. Wilde,' she stormed angrily. 'I wouldn't marry you if you were the last man on earth!'

Then she became aware of the speculative glances of the whole room, all the men who had stopped eating their breakfasts to watch what was happening, and with a half-sob she turned and ran desperately out of the canteen.

She sped across the compound and reached her bungalow breathless and sobbing. She ran inside, inserted the bolt on the door, and going into her bedroom she flung herself on the bed, tears streaming in angry humiliation down her cheeks.

# CHAPTER SEVEN

NICOLA did not leave her room again until the evening of that day. She wasn't hungry, and as for going into the office, well, she didn't particularly care whether Jason Wilde's reports were typed or otherwise. She knew he would probably have left the camp to go about his usual duties, but there would be Graham Wilson to face, and he was bound to be curious about the engagement and the subsequent argument in the canteen.

But by the time night had fallen she knew she could no longer remain in solitary confinement. Sooner or later she would have to face the men, and better to act naturally than skulk away in some corner arousing even more speculation. Even so, it took a great deal of courage to wash and make up her face and do her hair, then walk the few yards to the canteen. She hesitated on the doorstep, but then pushed open the door and went in.

For a moment, conversation lapsed as all eyes turned in her direction, but then the men seemed to sense her embarrassment and for once reacted to it favourably, turning back to their companions and beginning to talk again.

Nicola walked the length of the room to her table, which lately she had occupied alone, and when Graham appeared with some dinner for her she accepted it gratefully. He looked thoughtfully at her, then pulled out the chair opposite and sat down.

'Are you okay?' he asked anxiously. 'You look pretty pale.'

'I'm fine,' she replied, more calmly than she was feeling. 'Wh – where is everybody?'

'If you mean Jason, he's not here.'

'Not – not here?' she echoed blankly. 'You mean – not dining here?'

Graham shook his head. 'No, not just that. He's left. Gone! Back to London!'

'What!' Nicola was horrified. 'You can't be serious.'

'Why not?'

'Well, I mean – he didn't say anything to me!'

Graham shrugged. 'I guess you didn't give him much chance. As I heard it that was quite an argument you had in here with him this morning.'

Nicola's appetite disappeared. 'You heard about that?'

'Of course. Hell, that was quite some blow you dealt him, dashing out of here like the original maiden in distress.' Graham grimaced. 'I mean – if you'd wanted to argue with him you might at least have chosen somewhere private.'

Nicola heaved a sigh, and pushed her plate aside. 'Why has he gone to London, then? Because of that?'

Graham lifted his shoulders. 'Well, he was on the phone to Sir Harold before he saw you this morning, so I hardly think it's likely.'

'I see.' Nicola's mind buzzed with the thoughts that this new situation created. Whether Jason's reasons for going to London were anything to do with her or not it seemed obvious that her name would crop up in the course of his conversations with Sir Harold and then. . . . She shook her head. He was already suspicious of her reasons for coming here. If Sir Harold regaled him with his own supposedly recent history, Jason would be absolutely livid. Particularly as he knew she was Louise's sister. Not only might he expose her and jeopardize her job into the bargain, but he might also try to see Louise and get the real truth from her. Nicola didn't imagine Louise would be able to keep something like that to herself, not if Jason really turned on the pressure.

She pressed her hands to her temples, trying to think, and Graham said, somewhat anxiously: 'What's wrong? Heck, Jason will be back in a couple of days. I'm sure everything will turn out all right.'

Nicola managed a weak smile. 'I wish I could be as certain,' she murmured disconsolately.

Graham stayed a little longer and then when one of the men beckoned him he excused himself and left her alone. After he had gone, Nicola picked scantily at her dinner and then, rising, left the canteen. Back in her own bungalow, she sat down to try and decide what was the best thing for her to do.

If she stayed here, as obviously Jason expected her to do, and waited for his return, what then? Whether or not he learned the whole truth was really becoming the whole issue, and what he would do when he found out. Her plans seemed to be doomed to failure. True, she was now his fiancée, but she could derive no comfort from that. He had proved by the way he had kissed her the other evening that he had no respect for her, and put in his position any man would have reacted the same. He wasn't attracted to her, and it didn't seem as though he ever would be, and she might just as well accept the fact and return home. If she lost her job, what of it? There were always plenty of vacancies for qualified shorthand-typists, and with the secretarial experience she had accrued she had no worries on that score. What did worry her was Louise's reaction to all this. She had set off with such confidence, such high hopes of giving Mr. Jason Wilde a nasty awakening, but all she had achieved was to make an enemy of him, and aroused within herself an awareness that made the emotion she had felt towards her fiancé, Michael Ellison seem a paltry thing by comparison. Of course, it was not love, she told herself impatiently, it was simply his indifference that had disturbed the balance of her emotions.

She went to bed quite early, and surprisingly slept almost at once. She awoke feeling exhausted, the sunlight outside the room like an inferno that she could not escape.

But she could escape, she told herself, as she bathed and dressed. There was nothing to keep her in Castanya any longer. She could pack her bags, borrow transport, and be in Gitana by lunch time. There was bound to be a flight today or tomorrow, and she didn't mind spending a night in a hotel in Gitana. There was quite a good one run by the airline, she could use that.

The decision made, she walked quite jauntily to breakfast, and ignored Graham's speculative stare, and the stares of the other men. She would have to tell Graham, of course. He would have to obtain transport for her, but she had no intention of telling him in the canteen with the whole crew looking on.

She ate a slice of toast, drank several cups of coffee, and felt ready for anything. Emerging from the building into the morning light, she breathed deeply. It seemed strange to imagine London. It might easily be raining there, people dashing to work through puddles, cars splashing would-be-bus-travellers as they waited in long queues. Of course, right now London would be still and silent, only the street cleaners grinding their way along the gutters.

She sighed. She would be sorry to leave Castanya. It had been an exciting interlude, and one which she would not easily forget.

As she began to walk across to the bungalow to gather her belongings together she heard the pound of hooves as she had once heard before, and swinging round, she saw the group of horsemen enter the streets of the camp. Recognizing Sheikh Ali Ben Abdul Mohammed, Nicola walked hastily towards the bungalow, but he had recognized her heavy swathe of honey-gold hair and came cantering up to her swiftly, preventing her escape.

'Ah, *mademoiselle*,' he murmured. 'It is a pleasure and a delight to see you. Where is Monsieur Wilde this morning?'

Nicola had the feeling that his question was slightly false, as though he already knew the answer. Of course, here, where the grapevine worked so vigorously, he would be bound to know that Jason was in London. A ripple of apprehension slid along her veins, and she answered:

'My – my fiancé is not here. He left for London early yesterday morning.'

'Indeed?' The Sheikh inclined his head as though confirming her words. 'He has gone and left his English rose behind?'

'My – my work is here,' she said, managing to sound cool and businesslike. 'Naturally, I am not a free agent. I could not accompany him.'

'So?' The Sheikh frowned. 'I find this surprising. I should have thought the gallant Monsieur Wilde would not wish to leave his so-beautiful fiancée behind here, in such a dangerous place.'

'Dangerous, Sheikh Mohammed?'

'But of course. The desert is always dangerous. Besides, at any moment the camp could be invaded by hostile tribesmen. Without your fiancé you are at the mercy of all manner of dangers.'

Nicola decided he was deliberately trying to alarm her. She was beginning to understand Jason's feelings towards this man, and so she merely smiled calmly, and said: 'I think you exaggerate, Sheikh Mohammed, but it was kind of you to be concerned about my health.'

The Sheikh inclined his head, studying her thoughtfully. 'And why has Monsieur Wilde gone to London, *mademoiselle?*' he queried.

'Your guess is as good as mine,' she returned smoothly. 'Now, if you'll excuse me, I have things to do.'

The Sheikh's horse reared a little as he drew it back, and for a moment Nicola thought he meant to trample her underfoot, then the moment passed and she was free to enter her bungalow. Inside, she sank down weakly on to a chair. There was something about that man that alarmed her in spite of her imminent departure.

She stayed discreetly behind the blinds and watched the Sheikh and his retinue canter up the street towards the office building and she saw Graham Wilson come out to speak to them. She sighed with relief. At least Graham was still here, and he always seemed very reliable.

Later, after the horses' hooves had pounded away, she drew out her suitcases and began to pack. It did not take her long. Most of her clothes had remained in the suitcases once she had learned that she was expected to wear trousers and shirts at all times. She stuffed makeup and toilet articles into a plastic bag, pushed sandals down into corners, checked that she had her money and passport and her return ticket to London.

She was about to go in search of Graham when there was a tap at her door. She called 'Come in,' and Graham himself entered the lounge, looking frowningly at her packed cases.

'What's going on?' he asked, at once. 'You're not leaving!'

Nicola nodded. 'Yes, I am, Graham. Will it be possible to arrange transport to Gitana? I can get a flight from there.'

Graham flung himself into a chair and cupping his chin on one hand surveyed her broodingly. 'I don't know whether I ought to let you do this,' he muttered gloomily. 'Jason said nothing about you going back to London.'

'What I'm doing has nothing to do with Jason Wilde,' replied Nicola sharply. 'I manage my own affairs, and I make my own decisions.'

Graham gave an exclamation. 'You're Jason's fiancée now, remember.'

Nicola's head jerked up. 'Who told you that?'

Graham sighed. 'Who do you think? Jason, of course.'

Nicola hesitated, looked thoughtful for a moment, and then shrugged. 'Oh, well, what of it? So far as he is concerned I'd as soon be in Timbuktu!'

'I don't believe that,' exclaimed Graham. 'Heavens, what's a quarrel? Sarah and I have them all the time.'

'Sarah's your wife?'

'Yes.' Graham grimaced. 'I wish she was here,' he muttered. 'I wouldn't be arguing with her.' He shrugged. 'Anyway, that doesn't help my problems.'

'You have problems? Why? Has the Sheikh created a new crisis?'

Graham grinned. 'You're catching on fast, aren't you, Nicola? Yeah, I guess you could say that. There's some trouble brewing about the number of barrels the

Sheikh is entitled to. Oh, it's kids' stuff. Not worth bothering about in the normal way. In fact, I'm pretty convinced the Sheikh only came here to make sure Jason was away, that's what worries me!'

Nicola frowned. 'But what could he do? I mean – well, Jason is bound to come back soon.'

'I know. But compared with him, I'm pretty poor stuff. Hell, the Sheikh knows that. It will be in his interests to incite unrest while Jason is away. While Jason is here he finds his hands more or less tied.'

'Don't underestimate yourself so much,' said Nicola, shaking her head. 'I'm sure you're just as capable as Jason Wilde.'

Graham shook his head. 'No, I'm not, and old Mohammed knows it.' He got to his feet. 'Look here, you're not serious about leaving, are you? I mean – well, at least stay until Jason returns. That way it's his responsibility, not mine.'

Nicola shook her head. 'I don't want to see Jason again, right now,' she said. 'I'm sorry, Graham. I suppose you'll bear the brunt of this, but at least let me make up my own mind.'

Graham sighed. 'Well, I can't exactly forbid you to leave, can I? As for transport, I guess Ali could drive you out to Gitana. He has Jason's Land-Rover while Jason is away. All the other vehicles are in use. Except that car of Paul Mannering's, of course.'

'Well, I'd rather not be responsible for that,' said Nicola, with a smile. 'The Land-Rover will do fine. If Ali will take me, of course.'

'Oh, he'll take you if I ask him. But look here,

Nicola, can't I persuade you in any way—'

'No, I'm sorry, Graham, but I want to go home. I've had enough of deserts and Sheikhs and oil-wells for the time being.'

'All right, all right. I'll go and see Ali about the Land-Rover. You probably won't get a flight out of Gitana right away, you know.'

'I know. But there's bound to be one tomorrow, or the next day. Either way, I'll manage.'

'Well, okay.' Graham looked reluctant, but there was nothing more he could say. He left to see about the transport, and Nicola gathered together her things and took a last look round the bungalow. It wasn't that she was nostalgic, or anything. It was just rather depressing to know that everything she had planned for had fallen so flat.

However, when Graham returned he had some bad news for her. 'The Land-Rover's developed an oil leak,' he said. 'Ali's working on it at the moment. He doesn't know how long it will take to fix.'

'Damn!' Nicola flopped down on to a chair. 'How long does he think?'

Graham shrugged. 'Not long, he hopes. He said he might have it fixed by lunch time.'

Nicola grimaced. 'Oh, well, I suppose that will have to do. That means I'll definitely not get a flight before tomorrow.'

'That's right.'

Nicola shrugged. 'Oh, well, I suppose I ought to be thankful it's not more serious,' she said. 'Thanks for telling me, Graham. Do you need my help this morning?'

'If you like.'

She nodded. 'Okay, I'll come over.'

The morning passed quite swiftly, and Nicola ate lunch with Graham in the canteen, listening to his conversation about his family back in Birmingham. He became very enthusiastic when he discussed his three children, and she envied him his apparent lack of problems.

Afterwards she walked across to Jason's bungalow and found Ali wiping his hands on an oily rag. He beamed when he saw Nicola.

'It is all fixed,' he announced proudly. 'There will be no more trouble!'

Nicola pondered the wiseness of making such a sweeping statement, but she smiled and nodded, and said: 'Have you eaten? Or are you ready to leave?'

'Ali is not hungry,' he replied firmly. 'Where are your suitcases?'

'They're at the bungalow. I'll get them.'

Ali shook his head. 'I will get them,' he said, pointing to himself ostentatiously. 'Are you ready?'

Nicola glanced round. 'I'll just tell Graham Wilson we're leaving,' she said, and Ali nodded his agreement.

It was strange how much of a pull leaving actually was when it came down to it. Perhaps it was because in spite of everything she had found a certain satisfaction in challenging Jason Wilde, and Castanya would always be synonymous with him. There was an awful empty feeling inside her when she contemplated his reactions when he found she had gone. Perhaps she had beaten him after all. At least he would be unable to come back and make mincemeat out of her as he no doubt expected to do.

The road to Gitana was flat and uninteresting, mile after mile of rough track edged by scrub grass and desert, undulating into the far distance. To the left rose the mountain range which she and Jason had crossed to reach Sheikh Mohammed's dwelling, while to the right lay the pipeline, like some ugly snake on the sand.

Ali was vociferous, talking about the job he had just done on the Land-Rover, the heat, and the possible date of completion of the pipeline. His chatter helped to dull the ache she was beginning to feel in the pit of her stomach, and she wondered how long it would take them to reach the coast. Finally he said:

'Mr Jason is not going to be pleased that you have left the camp, Miss King.'

Nicola's eyes widened. 'Oh, no?'

'No. I told Mr. Wilson this also. I am not at all sure whether I ought to be the one who is taking you to Gitana. Things will not go well with me if Mr. Jason is angry.'

Nicola smiled. 'I'm sure you can handle it, Ali,' she replied easily. 'You seem capable of handling most things.'

'Yes, but Mr. Jason is different,' insisted Ali, with a slightly mournful expression. 'He can be very angry.'

Nicola grimaced. 'I know. Never mind, tell him it was all my fault.'

Ali raised his eyes heavenward. 'I do not think that will matter to Mr. Jason. I will be wrong just the same.'

Nicola frowned. 'It's rather late to have this attack of conscience, isn't it?' she asked. 'I mean, you didn't seem at all concerned back at Castanya.'

'It was the oil leak,' he said, screwing up his face and nodding. 'Yes, most definitely it was the oil leak. I was so pleased to have fixed it, I forgot everything else.'

Nicola chuckled. 'Oh, Ali,' she exclaimed, 'you are a fool!'

Ali grinned tentatively, as though trying it out, and then his dark face creased into laughter. 'Yes, yes, I think that is what I am,' he chortled.

After that they were silent for a while, each busy with their own thoughts. They were approaching a kind of pass between two outcrops of rock, and the heat was intense. Nicola fanned herself rather languidly, wishing she had had the courage to ask Ali to travel at night.

'Could we stop for a while?' she asked, wiping her forehead with her handkerchief. 'I'm roasting.'

Ali shrugged, looking about him thoughtfully. 'This is not a good place to stop, Miss King,' he said doubtfully. 'These rocks can be the hiding place for bandits.'

'Bandits!' Nicola ridiculed the idea. 'I've never heard of such a thing. Are you scared, Ali?'

'Me scared? Ali scared?' Ali stuck out his chest. 'Ali is not scared of anything.'

Nicola looked exasperated. 'Well, then?'

Ali hesitated, and then, just as Nicola was about to command him to stop, they both saw the body of a man lying on the road in front of them. Ali swung the wheel of the Land-Rover as though to bypass the body, but Nicola looked horrified as his actions revealed his intention.

'You can't just drive past!' she exclaimed. 'Heavens, he might be ill – or needing water or something. Stop at once!'

Ali slowed but he did not immediately stop. 'I would rather not, Miss King,' he insisted. 'The man will survive. The sun will be going down soon. He will reach water, if indeed he is needing it.'

'Oh, don't be so ridiculous!' snapped Nicola angrily. 'You simply can't leave a man lying in the middle of the desert alone like that!'

Ali was forced to bring the car to a halt. 'He may not be alone,' he hissed at her dramatically. 'I tell you there are bandits around here.'

'Oh, nonsense!' exclaimed Nicola, and slid determinedly out of her seat.

She walked back to where the man lay. He was lying on his stomach, and seemed completely unconscious. She knelt down beside him and gently turned him over. He looked harmless enough, although there was something vaguely familiar about his features. She frowned. She was imagining things. She didn't know any Arabs to recognize any of them.

She stood up and beckoned Ali, who had remained cautiously by the Land-Rover. 'Bring the water bottle,' she called. 'Quickly!'

Ali stared at her, looked as though he was about to object, and then with a muttered curse leant inside the vehicle and retrieved the plastic water container. Looking about him apprehensively, he made his way to her side, and bent down beside the Arab. As he did so, the Arab's fist shot upwards in a brutal movement, his blow all the more severe because it met Ali's head as it was in the process of coming down. Ali's neck cracked alarmingly, and with a groan he fell to one side.

It had all happened so unexpectedly that Nicola did not have time to make any kind of defence. As Ali fell the Arab sprang to his feet and grasping her arms imprisoned them behind her back.

Nicola gave an involuntary scream, and almost as though called by her protest, several more Arabs appeared from behind the rocks, leading horses. And then Nicola realized why the Arab who had lain prostrate on the ground had looked so familiar. He was the man who had assisted Sheikh Ali Ben Abdul Mohammed to mount and dismount from his horse.

'Are you mad?' she gasped, trying to free herself. 'What's the idea?'

The man, who had been holding her securely, handed her over to one of his colleagues, and came round to face her. 'We are not mad, Miss King,' he said, in perfect English. 'It is at the orders of Sheikh Mohammed that we have apprehended you here. Do not be alarmed, however. We mean you no harm. But we have been instructed to escort you to our master.'

'To Sheikh Mohammed?' Nicola exclaimed, an awful sense of fear overwhelming the anger she had first experienced.

'Yes, that is so.'

Nicola looked down at Ali, who was slowly coming round. 'But I'm on my way to Gitana. I – I leave for England tomorrow.'

'I cannot discuss anything with you, Miss King,' replied the man suavely. 'It is not my concern. I have my orders, and they will be carried out, of this you can be assured.'

Nicola needed no reassuring on that score. With Ali almost helpless, and her own predicament even worse, they didn't stand a chance. 'Wh-what about Ali?' she managed to whisper.

'You mean this man?' The Arab kicked Ali with a careless foot. 'Do not alarm yourself on his account. He will be accompanying us.'. Then he uttered something in the fast Arabic Nicola had heard some of the men about the camp use, and one of the Arabs went to climb into the Land-Rover, and starting its engine, drove it up to them.

The Arab who was holding Nicola urged her not ungently into the vehicle, the back this time, and then he and the Arab who had done all the talking climbed in beside her. Ali was lifted unceremoniously and dumped in the back too, on the floor, and as the vehicle began to move one of the men secured his wrists and ankles with a strong cord.

Nicola sighed. She was helpless and pure unadulterated panic was threatening to grip her being. She could think of no reason why Sheikh Mohammed should seek to kidnap her like this unless he had plans for her which she would personally find repulsive. And the chances of their whereabouts being discovered were slight indeed. Ali would not be due back from Gitana for at least twenty-four hours, and even then it was doubtful whether a search party would be mounted immediately just to search for one errant Arab servant. And in any case, a lot could happen in twenty-four hours.

The Land-Rover jerked and bumped uncomfortably over roads that were never meant for engine-driven vehicles. The heat in the back of the vehicle was stifling, and that combined with the smell of the men's sweaty bodies was enough to nauseate Nicola had not her own precarious situation instilled her with enforced strength. Once Ali looked up at her and said: 'I'm sorry, Miss King,' in his peculiarly educated tones, but he only got another kick for his trouble and Nicola refrained from answering him in case it caused him more bother.

The journey seemed endless, and she realized they were heading towards Abyrra. Her heart sank. She remembered the Sheikh's residence, the thick walls, the airless atmosphere, the guarded courtyard. Once there her chances of escape would be slight indeed.

The Land-Rover halted at the gates of the Sheikh's dwelling, which Nicola could see now resembled a kind of palace with its cupolas and minarets. The Arab urged her out again, and she jumped down on to the sand, wondering why the Land-Rover was not taking them to the courtyard at least. But that much at least became evident. After they had alighted, the Arab who was driving drove off, accompanied some distance behind by one of the riders who had followed them back over the mountains.

'The vehicle will be found abandoned,' explained the Arab as Nicola stared at the disappearing cloud of dust. 'It would not do for tracks to be found here, Miss King. Now come, the Sheikh is waiting.'

Nicola hesitated. 'Ali—' she began. The poor man was lying inert on the sand, unable to move from where he had been thrown.

'He will be attended to. Come,' retorted the Arab imperiously, and Nicola was forced to accompany him. Her nerves were stretched to fever pitch, and she felt sick with fear. She who had always imagined herself the mistress of any situation had now found herself wanting.

# CHAPTER EIGHT

THE Sheikh Abi Ben Abdul Mohammed awaited her
in his conference chamber, lounging lazily on his
cushions studying a problem set out on a chess board in
front of him. The chessmen were made of ivory and in
spite of her predicament Nicola could not help but
admire the intricacy of their design. He looked up at
her entrance and a smile enveloped his dark face.

'Ah, Mademoiselle King,' he murmured, getting to
his feet. 'I am delighted you decided to honour us by
your presence.

'I didn't have much choice,' returned Nicola shortly,
summoning all her courage. She must not let this man
see she was frightened or she might just as well succumb to whatever plans he had for her. She sensed the
Sheikh was a man who would admire spirit in a
woman. He would be too used to the fawning ob-
eisance practised by his own women.

The Sheikh inclined his head now in acknowledg-
ment of her statement, and then smiled. 'Nevertheless,
we are pleased to have you here.' He snapped his
fingers and a servant appeared immediately. 'Some refreshment for our guest,' he said brusquely, and the
man withdrew bowing low. 'Won't you sit down?' The
Sheikh indicated a place beside him, but Nicola deliberately chose to sit at the furthest point from him, and
he made no objection. Seating himself, he said: 'Are

you not curious to know why I have brought you here?'

Nicola's nails dug into the palms of her hands, but when she spoke she instilled indifference into her voice. 'Your motives cannot be reasonable ones,' she said, 'and I do not particularly care to make conversation with a man who by his very actions belies his status as ruler of Abrahm.'

'Why do you think my motives are unreasonable?'

Nicola shrugged. 'Because of the manner in which I was brought here. Kidnapping is not exactly legal, is it?'

The Sheikh half-smiled. 'For a woman in your precarious position, you are remarkably untroubled,' he said. 'But I admire your spirit.'

Nicola compressed her lips. There seemed nothing to say. The Sheikh offered her a cigarette and when she refused he lit one for himself. Then he leant forward and said:

'What if I told you you had enchanted me? That I could not rest until you were mine!'

Nicola's cheeks paled a little, but she held up her head defiantly. 'I wouldn't believe you,' she replied clearly.

The Sheikh stared at her for a moment, and then he burst out laughing. 'Oh, Miss King, you do not realize how refreshing it is for me to speak to someone who does not immediately begin to bore me with their insufferable humility!' He lifted his shoulders. 'It may be that you are right, my motives for bringing you here were not what I suggested, but with every passing minute I begin to wonder whether indeed I am wasting my opportunities.'

Nicola stiffened. 'Please,' she said, 'get to the point.'

The Sheikh drew deeply on his cigarette. 'You are impatient, *mademoiselle*. For that I think you must wait a little bit longer. See, here is some refreshment. I have ordered tea – that is what you English enjoy most of all, is it not?'

Nicola stifled a ready retort. It would not do to annoy the Sheikh. Amusing him was one thing, arousing his anger was quite another. He was too unpredictable to state with any certainty what his reactions might be.

The tea was very un-English. There was no sugar or cream, only lemon, and Nicola scalded her mouth in her impatience to get the ceremony over with. The Sheikh spent his time studying her, and she was half afraid to drink the liquid in case it contained some kind of narcotic. But, whatever happened, she could not improve her position by refusing his hospitality, so she drank the tea, ate a tiny sticky sweetmeat, and waited for the Sheikh to satisfy her curiosity.

Eventually the Sheikh tired of the delay himself and summoned a servant to clear the cups and dishes away. When all was tidy again, he said:

'Now, I will tell you why I have brought you here, Miss King. To begin with, you need not alarm yourself, no harm will come to you providing Monsieur Wilde does as I want him to do.'

Nicola's eyes narrowed. 'What do you mean?'

'I mean that your Monsieur Wilde is getting – how shall I put it – in my hair! He annoys me, and I do not wish him to annoy me any longer. Too much is at stake.'

Nicola summoned her scattered wits. 'You don't imagine I am important to Jason Wilde, do you?' she exclaimed.

The Sheikh smiled. 'Thank you, *mademoiselle,* for confirming my suspicions.'

'What do you mean?' Nicola was perplexed.

The Sheikh shrugged, smoothing the soft material of his robe. 'I never believed that Jason Wilde was your fiancé, Miss King, but on the other hand I could not prove otherwise. Now you have told me yourself. It is as I suspected. You are not Monsieur Wilde's responsibility, except inasmuch as he is responsible for all the crew at Castanya. You came out here with Paul Mannering. Oh, I admit it was a clever idea pretending to be involved with Wilde, but all along I suspected that Sir Harold's son was your real attachment.'

Nicola stared at him in amazement. 'You can't be serious!' she exclaimed. 'Oh, you can't be serious!'

'Why not?'

'Because I'm nothing to Paul! Heavens, he's two years younger than I am!'

'What of it? Age is nothing. And there must be some serious attachment for Sir Harold to allow you to accompany his son to such a place as Castanya! Or maybe you came for kicks. It is not unknown. I have heard of rich young women doing all manner of strange things for amusement.'

'I'm not a rich young woman!' gasped Nicola.

The Sheikh shrugged. 'That is of no matter. Your own importance lies not in your wealth, but in your involvement with Paul Mannering. I do not think even Sir Harold Mannering would accept a situation where your – shall we say – future was in jeopardy. I can imagine it might cause quite a scandal, and it would not be unreasonable for Abrahm to break off diplomatic relations with a country who accuses us of such a liberty as to kidnap the fiancée of the chairman of Inter-Anglia Oil's son.'

'Oh, that's ridiculous!' exclaimed Nicola, shaking her head wildly. 'I tell you, I'm nothing to the Mannerings. I didn't come out here to be with Paul. I came out—' She halted abruptly.

'Yes?' The Sheikh was leaning towards her. 'Just why did you come out here, Miss King? I do not believe you can convince me that your position here in Abrahm is not of importance to somebody.'

Nicola sought about for words. 'Of course my position here is important to somebody. To my sister. But I hardly think that constitutes an international incident, Sheikh Mohammed!' she exclaimed hotly. 'All right, all right, I'll tell you why I'm here. I came out to Castanya for one reason, and one reason only, to get even with Jason Wilde for what he did to my sister. She was happily married when he came along and smashed her happiness by making her so infatuated with him that she deserted her husband. I was engaged to her husband's brother and in the circumstances my engagement was broken, too!' She rubbed the back of her hand across her cheeks. 'Does that answer your question? Right now, Jason Wilde is in London finding out how I've cheated him! Do you imagine he'll give a damn what happens to me?' She sighed. 'As for Sir Harold Mannering, I doubt whether he'll even remember my name.'

The Sheikh's brows were drawn together in an angry frown. 'You cannot prove this, Miss King,' he snapped. 'I do not believe you.'

Nicola smoothed back her hair, and as she did so she remembered the letter she had received from Louise. 'Yes, I can,' she exclaimed. 'Where is my handbag? If you can fetch me that I can show you a letter that proves what I've said is the truth!'

The Sheikh stared at her and then he snapped his fingers impatiently. When the servant appeared he ordered him to fetch Nicola's bag, and then while they waited, he said:

'If what you say is true, if you can prove what you say, then you realize you are of no importance to me either. How do you know I will not dispose of you for my trouble?'

Suddenly Nicola's fear left her. She gave a slight smile. 'Because I believe you are not a vicious man,' she said, shrugging. 'I don't think you will kill me just to satisfy your anger at this mistake. Besides, you said I had spirit. Would you quench that spirit for speaking out?'

The Sheikh's expression softened a little. 'You are a brave young woman, Miss King.' He nodded. 'And what you say has truth in it. I do not think I will dispose of you after all.'

Nicola moistened her lips. 'Are you threatening me with banishment to your harem?' she asked.

The Sheikh lifted his shoulders. 'Perhaps.'

'Then I don't think you should do that either,' said Nicola carefully. 'I would be an unsettling influence among your wives. Just imagine the furore I might create! What you admire in me as spirit could become rebellion with so many supporters.'

The Sheikh's face relaxed completely, and he laughed. 'Oh, Miss King, you are indeed an unusual young woman. And one I will not soon forget.'

The servant appeared with the handbag, and the Sheikh indicated he should hand it to Nicola. When she would have opened it to take out the letter, he held up his hand. 'That will not be necessary,' he said firmly. 'I have had time to think, and I have decided I believe your story. No one who has such confidence in themselves could be lying.' He snapped his fingers again. 'Mamoud! Tell Khalif to bring my car to the door. Miss King will be leaving in a few minutes.'

Nicola could hardly believe it. The Sheikh's words about her confidence rang a little hollowly inside her. Had he but known it, she was a trembling mass of nerves within. She got unsteadily to her feet and the Sheikh said: 'Yes, Miss King, you can go. I do not doubt that you will get even with Monsieur Wilde. I do not envy him.'

Nicola managed a smile. 'I would like to thank you for your – your understanding,' she said.

'You thought I was merely a savage, is that right?'

the Sheikh smiled.

Nicola lifted her shoulders. 'I didn't know what to think.'

'So now perhaps you will take pleasant memories home with you to England,' murmured the Sheikh gently. 'Come, I will escort you to the car. My chauffeur will see that you complete your journey to Gitana and make sure you reach England in safety.'

Nicola was amazed at the opulence of the vehicle which awaited her. While Mamoud stowed her cases into the boot, the Sheikh spoke in rapid Arabic to the driver, and Nicola wondered what was being said. Even now, she felt a slight distrust of the Sheikh although she was convinced he meant what he said when he told her she was as good as home. Then she remembered Ali.

'My – my driver,' she exclaimed. 'What of him?'

The Sheikh frowned. 'I will see that tomorrow he is dispatched back to Castanya. Do not worry, *mademoiselle*. He will not be harmed either.'

Nicola bit her lip, and with this she had to be content. She could hardly insist that Ali accompany her to Gitana, and besides, the sooner he was returned to Castanya, the sooner her own position would be made clear. At least no one would have to worry about her safety that way.

She climbed into the sleek automobile, accepted the Sheikh's salute, and then nodded to Khalif that she was ready to leave. It was dark now and only the realization that what she was leaving behind was far worse than the journey ahead of her consoled her exhausted senses.

After all, Khalif was in the pay of the Sheikh, and she had nothing to fear.

Whether exhaustion overwhelmed her, or whether indeed there had been some kind of narcotic in the tea, she didn't know, but soon after they set off, her head drooped tiredly, and in no time at all she was asleep.

She was awakened by the sound of music and activity, and she sat up with a start to see that they were driving along streets where even at this time of night there was plenty of action. Neon-lighted arcades advertised their shoddy wares while beat music combined with the shrill wail of reed-pipes issued from every open doorway. She realized it was the dock area of Gitana. She and Paul had driven along here from the airport.

She glanced at Khalif. 'I must have slept the whole way!' she exclaimed.

Khalif nodded. 'Yes, *mademoiselle*. We are going to the harbour. The Sheikh's yacht awaits you there.'

'*Yacht!*' Nicola sat bolt upright in her seat. 'But – but if you take me to the hotel I can wait until tomorrow and get a flight. I don't need a yacht!'

'Sheikh Mohammed's orders,' returned Khalif implacably, and Nicola seethed with annoyance. Her sleep had restored some of her resilience, and now she felt indignant that she should have been duped in this way.

'Am – am I not to be allowed to return to England after all?' she exclaimed. 'So much for your Sheikh Mohammed's words!'

Khalif gave her a disdainful stare. 'The Sheikh Ali Ben Abdul Mohammed will keep his word,' he replied coldly. 'There are no flights out of Abrahm for the next thirty-six hours. The yacht will take you along the coast to Tripoli where there are regular flights to Rome and from there to London.'

'Oh!' Nicola pressed a hand to her throat. 'I – I didn't understand.'

'Obviously not. However, you may rest assured your return to England is guaranteed.'

Nicola didn't know what to say, but when she saw the magnificent equipage of the Sheikh's yacht she relaxed and found enjoyment in being treated like a royal personage. The Captain of the yacht was French, a man in his fifties who was kind and sympathetic when Khalif made known his master's instructions. Nicola was welcomed aboard and no questions were asked. Apparently Khalif was to accompany her to Tripoli, and she wondered rather doubtfully whether everything was going to be as simple as he made it out to be. Thoughts of white slave-trafficking, narcotic smuggling and arms smuggling flooded her brain, but in fact she had nothing to fear. The voyage was completed in comfort, and transport was waiting for them to escort Nicola to the airport. Obviously the ship's radio had been used to relay the Sheikh's instructions in advance and all the arrangements went smoothly. Too smoothly, thought Nicola, but she could find no complaints to register.

Instead, she was able to leave everything in Khalif's hands, and if some rather strange glances were cast in their direction, she ignored them. After all, no one knew her identity or that of Khalif, and his rather outlandish mode of dress was accepted as normal here. Even so, it was not until the B.O.A.C. VC-10 rose majestically from the tarmac at Idris El Awal that she felt really safe again.

Back in London yet another surprise awaited her. It was late in the evening when she finally took a taxi to the flat which Louise had come to share with her in St. John's Wood. A steady drizzle was falling, and Nicola felt cold and miserable and tired, not really willing to discuss her unexpected return with anybody, least of all with the man who opened the door to her.

'George!' she exclaimed, stepping inside, and dropping her suitcases tiredly on the floor. 'What are you doing here?'

Louise came bustling out from the lounge. She was in her dressing gown, and there was an embarrassed, flustered expression on her face. George was in his shirt-sleeves, and from their appearance they had certainly not spent the evening rowing with one another.

'Nicola!' exclaimed Louise, in astonishment. 'What are you doing here? Why didn't you let us know you were coming back?'

Nicola grimaced at George, and then walked tiredly into the living room. Here there was more evidence of George's occupation. His slippers stood beside the fire, his pipe lay on the mantelpiece, his monthly motoring magazine was lying on a chair, as though he lived there.

Nicola swung round. 'I think I should have let you know I was coming,' she exclaimed, half angrily. 'What's going on, Louise? Two and a half weeks ago when I left here you were lonely and depressed. Your marriage with George was over. Now I come back unexpectedly and find George here, obviously in residence. Don't you think I'm entitled to some explanation?'

George glanced at Louise who was wringing her hands, and then said: 'Sit down, Nicola. Louise, go and make some tea. Your sister looks worn out.'

Nicola did as he suggested and flung herself into a chair, kicking off her shoes. She was tired and fed-up, and George's amiable, plump features were not the ones she wanted to see. She had expected Louise to be glad to see her, sorry that she hadn't achieved anything, but glad to see her anyway. Now she felt like an interloper in her own flat.

After Louise had left the room, still looking anxious, George seated himself opposite his sister-in law and said: 'Well, Nicola, I suppose I must tell you what's been happening.'

'Yes, George, I think you must,' said Nicola blankly.

George lifted his pipe off the mantel and began to fill it thoughtfully. It was his way of avoiding her eyes, and she said, impatiently: 'Oh, for goodness' sake, George, get it out and get it over with!'

'All right.' George looked up at her. 'The day after you left – or maybe a couple of days after you left,' he amended, flushing slightly, 'Louise rang me up.'

'She did what!'

'She rang me. up. At work. She told me you had gone out to Abrahm on a job and she was alone with the children, and if I wanted to come and see them, I could.'

'I see.' Nicola shook her head, digesting this. She felt betrayed. From George's words she felt sure Louise had phoned him the minute she had left the country. But why? If she had wanted to phone him, why hadn't she done so before this?

Louise appeared in the doorway. 'Oh, Nicola,' she said uncomfortably, 'I'm sorry.'

Nicola kicked an unoffending newspaper aside with her foot. 'Oh, for heaven's sake, Louise,' she said shortly, 'don't say that! I just wish you'd phoned him before I left, that's all.'

'I – I wanted to,' began Louise.

'You what!' Nicola began to feel angry.

'I – I wanted to, Nicola. But you were always so strong-minded, so certain you were right, that I hadn't the heart to tell you that I wanted to go back to George.'

Nicola was furious now. 'How can you stand there and say such things!' she gasped. 'Why, only in that letter you sent you—'

Louise interrupted her. 'Now don't go getting George involved in your job,' she said quickly. 'George knows nothing about that!'

Nicola stared at her, and comprehension of what Louise was trying to convey swept over her. 'You mean—' she began slowly.

'I mean George and I have got over our upset, and we're going to give our marriage another try.'

'What!' Nicola stared at her sister incredulously. 'You can't have made up your mind to that so suddenly.'

'No, well, a lot of water has flowed under the bridge since last year. I'm a bit older and wiser now. I know that George and I have got to try again for the children's sake.'

Nicola got to her feet. She felt like bursting into tears. This was the last straw. She shook her head angrily and said: 'And why are you still here? I mean — why haven't you gone back to the house?'

'Because I've sold it,' said George, at once. 'We were never happy in that house. Besides, the children need more freedom than they have here in London. I've got a new job, it's in Coventry, we've got a new house there with a big garden. We expect to move in at the end of the month. We've stayed here because we had nowhere else to go. We didn't think you'd mind, being out of the country and all.'

Nicola looked astounded, and Louise hurried on: 'I — I was going to write to you, Nicola—'

'Decent of you,' snapped Nicola abruptly.

'Well, you know how it is. Time goes by so quickly,' exclaimed Louise miserably. 'Oh, Nicola, don't be angry. I'm sorry if I've spoiled all your plans.'

Nicola shook her head. 'You've spoiled no plans of mine, Louise,' she retorted. 'Oh, hell, I'm going to bed. We'll talk about this in the morning. I'm worn out.'

She noticed that neither of them seemed particularly

interested in why she had come back so abruptly, and she felt bitter and upset. This, on top of everything else, was too much.

'Er – I'll go and see about a bed,' began Louise, biting her lip.

'Oh, of course. George will be sleeping in your room,' muttered Nicola. 'Don't bother, Louise. There's the divan in the children's room, that will do for me.'

'Are you sure, Nicola?' Louise looked anxious.

'Of course I'm sure,' said Nicola, lifting one of her cases and carrying it through to the spare bedroom which the children had been using. 'Good night!'

'Oh, Nicola, you are angry,' wailed Louise, tears beginning to slide down her cheeks.

Nicola raised her eyes heavenward. 'No,' she denied swiftly. 'No, not angry, just depressed, that's all. Forget it. I'll see you both in the morning.'

But once she had climbed between the sheets of the narrow little divan, Nicola felt tears on her own cheeks. Somehow everything she had planned and worked for had rebounded on her in the most horrible way possible, and she just wanted to sleep and sleep, and forget everything and everybody. Somehow here, back in her own flat in London, the previous twenty-four hours had assumed the proportions of a dream, and only Jason Wilde and the anger he would reveal when he found she had cheated him yet again made any sense.

# CHAPTER NINE

THE next morning Nicola slept late and was awakened at ten by Louise bringing her in a cup of tea. Nicola slid up her pillows and accepted the tea gratefully, saying:

'Where are the children?'

Louise seated herself on the side of Nicola's bed. 'I took them out early on so that they wouldn't disturb you,' she replied. 'They're off to school now. George has gone to the office, so there's only you and me.'

Nicola sipped the hot tea. 'Well, you're looking more yourself,' she said uncomfortably, wishing Louise would stop looking at her as though she was suddenly going to explode or something.

Louise sighed. 'Oh, Nicola, I feel terrible!' she exclaimed.

'*You* feel terrible!' Nicola shook her head. 'How do you think I feel? Last night I felt as though it was all my fault that you and George had stayed separated for almost a year. Why ever didn't you tell me you wanted to go back to George, Louise? Heavens, I'd have been delighted!'

Louise shrugged her shoulders. 'I know, I know.'

'As it is you've made me out as some kind of a monster to George!' Nicola gathered anger as she spoke. 'Honestly, Louise, you deserve everything you get! And to cap it all, you didn't even tell George why I'd gone out to Abrahm. You've made it look as though I deserted you and the children, and you took the first opportunity of breaking away from me!'

Louise compressed her lips. 'Oh, Nicola, try to understand. You've got nothing to lose in all this. You're still free and heartwhole. I don't believe you ever really loved Michael, you got over it too quickly for that. I think your pride was damaged that's all, and that's why you went out to Abrahm, to try and restore your confidence in yourself as much as to get even with Jason Wilde.'

Nicola stared at her sister disbelievingly. 'Heavens, do you really believe that, Louise?' she gasped. Then, finishing her tea, she lay back on her pillows. 'Well, anyway, it doesn't really matter now. You're going to make a second start with George, and I got absolutely nowhere.'

Louise rubbed her nose thoughtfully. 'I suppose I'll have to tell you, Jason was here a couple of days ago.'

'*What!*' Nicola pushed herself up on her elbows. 'Here? In London, you mean?'

'No, I mean here. At the flat.'

Nicola swallowed hard. 'Oh, stop messing about, Lou,' she exclaimed. 'What – what did he want?'

'He wanted to see me,' replied Louise, standing up and walking across to the window. 'I thought that would surprise you.'

'Surprise me?' Nicola shook her head. 'No, it doesn't actually surprise me. What did he say?'

Louise leaned back against the window frame. 'He

wanted to know why you had persuaded Sir Harold Mannering to let you go out to Abrahm.'

Nicola flopped back on the pillows. 'And what did you say?'

Louise shrugged. 'I told him I didn't know.'

'And he accepted that?' Nicola looked sceptical.

'Not exactly. He said he had spoken to Sir Harold and he had a pretty good idea now why you had gone.' She looked softly reminiscent. 'He's a gorgeous male, isn't he?' She sighed. 'I could have fallen for him all over again.'

Nicola felt exasperated. 'So he just said that and went?' she questioned tersely.

'What? Oh, no, not exactly. I – er – I invited him in – for coffee. It was rather exciting talking over old times.'

'My God!' Nicola raised her eyes heavenwards. 'What did you talk about?'

Louise looked disgruntled. 'Well, you, mostly,' she admitted, rather irritatedly. 'Honestly, he wanted to know everything about you. Even about Michael.'

'So you told him?' Nicola was aghast.

'Of course. Why not? After all, it's nothing to him.'

'Exactly, so why tell him?' Nicola slid impatiently out of bed. 'Oh, Louise, the trouble you can cause!'

Louise walked haughtily to the door. 'If you're going to continue being insulting I shan't even bother to be polite,' she said angrily. 'It's not my fault that things didn't go right for you in Abrahm.'

Nicola breathed out in a low whistle. 'All right,

Louise, all right. I'm sorry if I'm not very polite, but quite honestly I don't feel very sociable this morning, and I'm beginning to wonder just what the relationship was between you and Jason Wilde. If he was the pig you made him out to be, how come you're offering him cups of coffee, and generally behaving as though he was some kind of gentleman?'

Louise halted by the door, holding the doorpost thoughtfully. 'Well, he wasn't such a beast. I mean, he didn't know I was married when he first took me out.'

Nicola swung round from her contemplation of her complexion in the dressing table mirror. 'But he knew later, didn't he?' she said sharply.

Louise shrugged, and then bent her head. 'Of course,' she replied shortly. 'Er – do you want any breakfast?'

Nicola shook her head and heaved a heavy sigh. 'No. Nothing for me, thanks.'

Louise bit her lip. 'You – you won't tell George about all this, will you? I mean, about Jason calling and everything.'

Nicola grimaced. 'Of course not. What do you take me for?'

Louise relaxed. 'Well, I'd hate anything to go wrong now. By the way, you haven't told me what happened in Abrahm, or why you've come home so abruptly. Was it something to do with Jason, or was it something else?'

Nicola shook her head 'I'll tell you later,' she said evasively. 'Right now, I've got a splitting headache.'

During the next few days, Nicola spent most of her time in the apartment. She occasionally took the children across to the park, and spent some time with them there, but mostly she stayed indoors, pretending the cold, frosty autumn weather was to blame.

She had expected Inter-Anglia would contact her. Sir Harold Mannering would know she was back in England by now, and she was surprised he had not attempted to get in touch with her. Unless what Jason had told him had digusted him so much that he had fired her on the spot and she might get her dismissal papers in the post at any time.

But nothing came and the days passed, and Nicola grew more and more depressed. She didn't exactly know what was depressing her, she only knew that she couldn't bear it if Louise tried to get her to discuss Jason Wilde or her life out in Abrahm. Somehow that period of her life was private and personal and she wanted no detailed examinations made of her actions by her sister. Somehow, her relationship with Louise had undergone a severe change, and Nicola found herself wondering whether she had been mistaken in thinking that Louise had wanted her to go out to Abrahm for any other reason than to give her time to contact George and try to persuade him to make another start at their marriage.

Louise's part-time job took her out of the flat during the afternoons, and it was this time that Nicola liked best. The children were at school, and George was at the office, and the place was quiet and peaceful, like it used to be before Louise's troubles began.

One afternoon, when she was making an attempt to clear out a cupboard, dressed in old slacks and a close-fitting sweater, the doorbell rang. Thinking it must be a tradesman or perhaps some friend of Louise's, Nicola went carelessly to the door, sweeping back her hair with one hand. When she opened the door, her heart somersaulted painfully, and a strange sickly feeling invaded her system.

'Jason,' she murmured, almost inaudibly. 'What – what are you doing here?'

Jason's face was set in hard lines, and there was a furious gleam in the depths of his dark eyes. 'My God!' he bit out savagely, 'you are here! What the hell do you think you're playing at?'

He thrust her back roughly into the hall, and entering the flat slammed the door behind him, leaning back against it and staring at her with burning eyes.

Nicola tried to gather her scattered senses. 'Wh-what are you talking about?' she gasped, pressing a hand to her throat.

Jason studied her silently for a few minutes, and then he seemed to relax a little. 'Aren't you going to invite me in?' he said harshly.

Nicola was trembling but indignant. 'You seem to be in,' she said unsteadily, and turning, she led the way into the living room where a warm fire burned in the grate.

Jason followed her, loosening the thick overcoat he was wearing over a dark suit. He looked tired, now she had a chance to examine his face more sensibly, and she wondered why he seemed so surprised to see her. Turning, she said:

'Do – do you want some coffee – or tea?'

Jason shook his head. 'No, thanks.' He surveyed her thoroughly. 'You can tell me what the hell has been going on, though.'

Nicola twisted her hands together. 'How do you mean?' she asked, frowning. 'I should have thought it was obvious to you why I haven't returned to the office. I should have thought you would be back in Abrahm by now.'

Jason stood, legs apart, hands in pockets, regarding her. Her cheeks burned. He still had the power to disturb her, and she was sure he was aware of it.

'I have been back to Abrahm,' he said tautly. 'Only to find you'd disappeared!'

'Disappeared?' Nicola frowned. 'Surely Ali told you what happened?'

'Ali? Oh, I see, you mean after the Sheikh kidnapped you.'

Nicola frowned. 'Well, of course. I mean – Sheikh Mohammed promised—'

'Do you believe his promises?' Jason was derisive.

Nicola sank down on to a chair. 'I think you'd better sit down and I'll explain how I got back to England,' she said. 'That is, if you really don't know.'

Jason refused to sit down, and Nicola felt immediately at a disadvantage. However, she went on: 'Where is Ali? Is he all right?'

Jason shrugged. 'Ali was found two days after you left, unconscious in the desert near Castanya. He was suffering from sunstroke. He's at present in hospital in

Gitana.'

'Oh, poor Ali!' Nicola felt contrite. 'Is he – was he able to talk?'

Jason moved restlessly. 'For God's sake, get on. Ali could tell us nothing after you disappeared into the Sheikh's palace.'

Nicola looked up at him. 'Didn't you get the message from Sheikh Mohammed?'

'Message? What message? We got no message! It wasn't until Ali was found that we entertained doubts as to your whereabouts. Graham rang London, and I took the next flight out.'

'I see.' Nicola was horrified. 'What happened?'

'I went to see Mohammed. There was no one else to contact after it was found you hadn't boarded any plane from Gitana.'

Nicola sighed. 'Oh, what a mess! That must have been—' She halted. Ought she to betray the Sheikh? He had at least made certain she was adequately set upon her journey.

'Yes?' Jason had heard her words. 'That must have been – what?'

Nicola frowned. 'Well, Sheikh Mohammed insisted I used his yacht to go along the coast to Tripoli, to save me hanging about in Gitana for a flight. I flew home from there.'

'I see.' Jason's voice was icily cool now. 'And didn't it occur to you to report to the London office, just to let us know your whereabouts?'

'No! That is . . .' Nicola sighed again. 'Oh, honestly, you must know why I left Castanya by now – why I didn't contact Sir Harold.'

Jason's eyes were intent. 'Oh, yes, I think I do,' he said tersely. 'Your intentions have been made quite clear. My consultations with Sir Harold and later with Louise were very revealing. However, as you've seen Louise no doubt she has explained that her own part in the proceedings was no innocent one.'

Nicola bent her head. 'She – well, we haven't discussed it in detail. She's going back to her husband. In fact, she's already gone back.'

'I know. I'm glad of that at least. I'd hate to have a broken marriage on my conscience, particularly that of your sister.'

Nicola got to her feet. 'Well, anyway, that's the whole story. I hope you're satisfied. I expect Sir Harold found it vastly amusing.'

Jason shrugged his broad shoulders. 'Harold knows no more than I've chosen to tell him,' he replied. 'So far as he's concerned, you chose to return to England of your own free will. Now that you're here, you're at liberty to take up your previous post, if you wish.'

Nicola stared at him. 'Are you serious?'

'Of course.'

Nicola shook her head. 'I suppose I should thank you.'

'Why? So far as you are concerned my intervention in your life was not a pleasing one. If it's any consolation I'm sorry I caused your engagement to be broken.'

Nicola smoothed her hair behind her ears. 'That's in the past now,' she murmured unevenly.

'Is it?' Jason studied her thoughtfully. 'So all this was really for Louise.'

'Of course.'

He shook his head. 'Such loyalty deserves to be rewarded,' he muttered, and as his eyes met Nicola's she felt a trembling sensation in her lower limbs. He moved towards the door, his thin face very serious for once, all mockery gone. 'If it soothes your injured pride at all, you can tell Louise you succeeded in your mission.'

Nicola stared at him. 'What do you mean?'

'What do you think I mean?' Jason's eyes were dark and enigmatic as ever.

'I don't know what to think,' she whispered shakenly.

'Then don't think at all,' he advised her softly, and opening the door he went out and closed it behind him.

Nicola stood staring at the door with tortured eyes. Had Jason really been here? Or had it all been a dream conjured up by her own desire to see him again? She shook her head. Of course he had been here. He had been searching for her. But the rest – those final words – he hadn't meant them, at least not in the way she wanted him to mean them.

And with this thought came the realization of why she had wanted him to mean them in that certain way. Her depression, this overwhelming sense of isolation had not been caused by Louise at all. She had not wanted to leave Castanya because Jason Wilde was there. And no matter how ridiculous it might be, and in spite of all the things she had known about him, she had reacted the same as all the other women, she had fallen in love with him, too.

She gave an involuntary sob. It couldn't be true. It mustn't be true. For even had he meant what he said, he was unlikely to sacrifice his bachelorhood for any woman, least of all one who had attempted to destroy him.

She went into the kitchen, busying herself with tasks to keep herself from thinking. She was glad now she had left Castanya when she did. Even if Jason had returned without betraying her she would not have been able to stand working with him, day in and day out, without betraying herself.

She lit a cigarette, and stilled her trembling nerves. When Louise returned home she was quite calm, and as Nicola's neighbour had thought it her business to tell Louise in passing that Nicola had had a visitor that afternoon, Louise came in all agog to know who it was.

Nicola lit another cigarette, and said, as flippantly as she could: 'If you must know, it was Jason Wilde.'

'Jason?' Louise raised her eyebrows. 'But I thought he told me he was going back to Abrahm.'

'He was. That is – he's been back, and returned to England again.'

'Why? Because you'd left?'

'Sort of. It's a complicated business.' Nicola noticed the way Louise's face had drawn in at this information, as though she was jealous. But she couldn't be jealous, thought Nicola, incredulously. And yet it seemed that she was.

'Anyway,' Nicola went on, 'it means I can go back to work for Sir Harold Mannering.'

Louise grimaced. 'So he didn't tell Sir Harold how you had insinuated yourself out there,' she said.

Nicola didn't like the word 'insinuated', but she let it go. 'More or less,' she agreed now. 'At any rate, it's sorted itself out.'

'Good. I'm pleased.' Louise shrugged. 'As it happens, George got to know this afternoon that the house will be ready in a week's time. So we'll be leaving. I wanted to know you were settled before we left.'

Nicola let this go too. She had the feeling Louise didn't much care about anybody but herself. But she enthused about the house, and agreed to go visiting as soon as they were straight. It was strange, listening to Louise talk about George so casually. A month ago his name was never mentioned.

Nicola sighed. Still, it was all over as she had said. Louise would settle down again, and the next time she got herself into trouble she could do her own extricating.

It wasn't until later that the whole weight of her own problems descended on Nicola, and she wondered how she would live once they were gone.

# CHAPTER TEN

NICOLA folded the last sheet of carbon into the sheaf of papers and inserted them into the typewriter. Then she opened the folder containing the information Sir Harold Mannering wanted transcribing and began to copy type. But her mind wasn't on her work. Since returning to the offices of Inter-Anglia Oil she had found it increasingly difficult to concentrate and now that Sir Harold had returned from his trip to South America she knew her task would be even more difficult.

It was a month since her return from Abrahm, and she had resumed her position as secretary to Sir Harold Mannering three weeks ago. But, fortunately for her peace of mind, Sir Harold was in the process of planning a trip to Brazil and he had left only a couple of days after her return to work. Before he left he had not troubled her with any personal questions, and she had been grateful, but now he had returned and there was no doubt that sooner or later he would want to know the whole story. It didn't matter that Jason hadn't revealed their real relationship, she would still have to explain what had occurred and why.

She sighed, and opening a packet of cigarettes, placed one between her lips. After it was lit, she exhaled gratefully, and lay back in her chair. Everything should have been as normal by now. Louise and

George had left for Coventry and were, as far as Nicola knew, settled there. Her life should have assumed its pattern, and she wished with a kind of desperation that she had never thought of going out to Abrahm. Had she accepted Michael's defection calmly, she would never have met Jason Wilde, never have succumbed to his arrogant personality, and would certainly never have involved herself in this mess of intrigue.

She started guiltily as the buzzer on her desk made its insistent noise. Pressing down the button, she said: 'Yes, Sir Harold?'

Sir Harold Mannering spoke charmingly to her: 'Nicola, come in here a moment, my dear.'

Nicola replied in the affirmative, and releasing the button got to her feet. The summons that she had been waiting for had come. She had somehow known it was imminent. Sir Harold had been back a few days and all the urgent work awaiting him on his return had been attended to.

Knocking on the door of the inner office which opened from her own, she entered a room furnished in the manner of all offices, except that as these offices were newly constructed everything was glass and Swedish wood, and very modern. Sir Harold rose from behind his desk at her entrance, and indicated that Nicola should sit in the chair opposite him. Nicola managed a smile, and subsided into the chair, and holding her notebook rather obviously in her hand she pretended to be waiting for dictation. Sir Harold noticed this.

'I'm sure you know it's time we had a talk,' he said

quietly. 'We haven't talked since your return, what with one thing and another. I didn't particularly want to go to South America, but I had no choice, and since I've been back there hasn't been a moment until now.'

Nicola placed her notebook resignedly on the desk in front of her. 'Yes, Sir Harold,' she said, rather stiffly.

Sir Harold frowned. 'Now, come along, Nicola, don't be frigid with me. You know very well that I expected something of this trip to Abrahm.'

Nicola sighed. 'I know, I know. And I'm sorry. But — well, Jason just doesn't want to know.'

'I can't believe that.' Sir Harold seated himself opposite her and lit a cigar. Drawing on it deeply he went on: 'When Jason came home here there was little question that he was involved with you, and seriously so. But he told me some story about you being jealous about another woman — somebody called Ellison, or something like that. At any rate, it was you and not he who had caused the rift, just as everything was developing nicely.'

Nicola was thankful to Jason for his tactful handling of that situation, but Sir Harold's words had involved her in a situation for which she was simply not prepared.

'I'm afraid Jason and I are just not compatible, after all,' she replied, flushing. 'All I seemed to do out there was cause him a lot of unnecessary bother.'

Sir Harold made an angry exclamation. 'Nicola, this doesn't sound like you at all. So subdued and spiritless! What's happened to you, girl? Has the hot sun of

Abrahm dried up all the hot blood in your veins?'

Nicola managed a smile. 'Oh, really, Sir Harold, I'd rather not discuss it.'

Sir Harold's fist thundered down on the table and she looked up in surprise. 'Honestly, Nicola, you infuriate me! A couple of months ago you couldn't wait to get out to Abrahm, you said you were dying to see Jason again. You were supposedly madly in love with him, and now – Good God! You're acting as though it was some milk-and-water affair that never got off the ground. I don't believe it! I just don't believe it! I know Jason – and I know you, and if he's been messing around with some other woman, then damn me! it must have been when you were quarrelling with him.' He got impatiently to his feet. 'If you'd seen him in here the day he couldn't lay hands on you, you'd have realized how stupid a word like "incompatibility" is! Have you any idea of the risks he ran trying to locate your whereabouts?'

Nicola stared at him. 'I don't know what you mean.'

'Don't you? Didn't he tell you he went to see Sheikh Mohammed? He said he did.'

'Oh, yes, he told me that.'

'But not in detail, I'll be bound. He made me promise not to broach this trouble about you leaving Abrahm like that, without contacting anyone, but dammit all, Nicola, I've got to mention it. Jason went through Sheikh Mohammed like a dose of salts!'

Nicola pressed a hand to her throat. 'How – how do you mean? I – I thought Sheikh Mohammed explained how he had taken me along the coast to Tripoli and had me flown home from there. How else did Jason know I was back in England?'

Sir Harold leant on the table, facing her. 'As I understand it, your precious Sheikh wouldn't say a word, not until Jason practically took him apart with his bare hands. Do you have any conception of the dangers to the company he ran by attacking Sheikh Mohammed like that? We could have been thrown out of the country – our equipment forfeited! And all because of you! As it was, all Jason got out of him was that you were to be found in England and if Jason hadn't found you I think Sheikh Mohammed would have suffered a fate worse than death!'

'Oh, heavens! I didn't know that.' Nicola shook her head. 'How terrible! So – so what has happened? I mean – has the company been forced out of Abrahm – or has Jason apologized – or what?'

'Jason? Apologize to Mohammed? You must be joking! No, as it happens things have been pretty quiet since then, ominously so. Any moment I'm expecting a telephone call to say that there's been more trouble.'

Even as he spoke the telephone rang, and Nicola lifted the receiver automatically, almost afraid of what she might hear. But it was merely one of the other directors wanting to speak to Sir Harold, and she handed him the receiver and rose to go.

'Wait!' Sir Harold put his hand over the mouthpiece so that their conversation would not be overheard. 'I'm flying out to Abrahm at the end of the week. Do you want to come with me?'

Nicola hesitated, stared at him longingly, and then shook her head. 'I – I don't think so, thank you,' she replied uncomfortably. 'After all, it's all over now. Me – Jason – everything. It's no good trying to kindle flames where none exist.'

Sir Harold looked as though he was about to argue, but obviously the director on the other end of the line was beginning to object to the delay, and with an angry dismissal, he started to talk to his colleague.

For the rest of the day, Nicola lived in a misery of longing. If only she could have gone out to Abrahm with Sir Harold, how wonderful that would have been. But she could not go running after Jason like that. If he had cared anything about her, why didn't he tell her so that day at the flat, instead of making ambiguous remarks which could not be taken seriously?

She sighed. Of course, she had given him no encouragement really, no reason for him to imagine she might conceivably be interested in him, particularly now as he had learned the real reasons for her trip to Abrahm. He might easily imagine that now that Louise had gone back to George, she would reunite with Michael again.

She sighed, and paced unhappily about the flat. She was home now, and still no happier about her feelings. If only he had given her a little encouragement, anything on which to base her hopes or fears. His comment about her having achieved her objective could mean anything. It could so easily mean that he was agreeable to her telling Louise something that was simply not true, just to save her face.

The night she spent was the longest she had ever known. She barely slept and was up at six, making herself coffee when the telephone rang. Frowning, she went to answer it, and found Sir Harold Mannering on the other end of the line.

'Nicola, is that you? Have I got you out of bed?'

'No, I was up.' Nicola frowned. 'What's wrong?' Even as she said the words, an awful premonition of disaster swept over her. 'Is it Jason?'

Sir Harold was swift to reassure her. 'No, nothing like that. But disturbing none the less. Nicola, there's been a revolt in Abrahm. The Gitana office phoned in half an hour ago. The army have taken control of the country, and deposed the Sheikh!'

'Oh, lord!' Nicola sank down weakly on to a chair, visions of gun battles that she had seen on television newsreels flooding her brain. 'How terrible! What about the – the – team?'

'That's what I'm phoning about. As far as I can gather it's been a bloodless *coup* and no one is hurt. But naturally, the communications are all dislocated, and it will be some time before order is restored. I'm ringing you because obviously this will appear in the late editions of the papers and I didn't want you to be alarmed on Jason's behalf. As you are, aren't you, Nicola? Deny it now, if you can!'

Nicola could not deny it. To imagine Jason injured or worse was anathema to her.

'Are – are you still going out to Abrahm at the end of the week?' she asked unevenly.

'No, today, but don't imagine you can change your mind and go now. I wouldn't take you into such a situation! Hell, anything could happen.'

'But – but I can't stay here,' murmured Nicola tremblingly. 'Oh, Sir Harold, don't make me!'

Sir Harold uttered a stifled curse. 'For God's sake, Nicola, don't cry. Look. Get dressed and get over here and we'll talk about it, right?'

Nicola agreed, and rang off; with shaking fingers she dressed and did her hair, and without bothering to wear any make-up she went out and grabbed a taxi. Sir Harold lived in an apartment in Belgravia, and it was here she directed the driver. Sir Harold was a widower, his wife had died some eight years previously, and Nicola knew that despite her denials at the time Jason was baiting her about her boss, she could have achieved almost anything with Sir Harold. It was only her supposed involvement with Jason that had forestalled his advances. Of course, he was much older than she was, already into his fifties, but he was a very impressive figure of a man and many a girl envied her her position as his secretary.

The taxi halted at the block of apartments and Nicola paid him hastily, and ran up the steps and into the building. A lift transported her to the penthouse, and soon she was ringing Sir Harold's doorbell.

Sir Harold's butler, Lewis, opened the door. He preferred the designation of butler, Sir Harold had told her, but actually he performed a great number of duties that did not come into that sphere.

'Come in, Miss King,' he said, smiling politely. 'Sir

Harold is expecting you.'

Sir Harold Mannering was in the huge lounge, pacing about restlessly smoking his usual cigar. He smiled warmly when he saw her and stopped his pacing to come to her side.

'Don't look so alarmed, Nicola,' he said. 'There's nothing to be alarmed about.'

Nicola shook her head. 'I'm sorry I look such a mess,' she said, indicating her attire of pants and anorak, hastily donned. 'I don't know what Lewis will think of me!'

Sir Harold looked down at her as though he enjoyed doing so. 'You look all right to me,' he said gently. 'Come and sit down. Lewis has prepared us some coffee, and there's even breakfast if you want it.'

'Oh, no, I'm not hungry,' she exclaimed, but she allowed him to lead her to the couch and they sat down together.

'So you want to come out to Abrahm?'

Nicola stared at him. 'Can I?'

Sir Harold shook his head slowly. 'No,' then as Nicola would have protested, he went on: 'Wait! I'm flying out this morning, via Palermo in Sicily. If you want to come with me, as far as Palermo, you can. At least that way I can fly back tonight and tell you what's going on.'

'You're flying to Gitana? But will there be any transport?'

'I'm using the company jet. We'll come down in Palermo to refuel! Well?'

Nicola could have hugged him. 'Oh – oh, of course.

180

You knew I'd say yes. Oh, Sir Harold, I don't know how to thank you.'

Sir Harold gave a rather wry smile. 'You do know,' he said softly. 'Either marry this arrogant brute, or me!'

Nicola's eyes widened. 'Why, Sir Harold—' she began.

'I know – I know. I'm too old,' he muttered, fingering a strand of her silky hair.

'No, I wasn't going to say that,' smiled Nicola, putting her hand over his. 'I'm grateful, that's all.'


Nicola sat on the balcony of the suite Sir Harold Mannering had taken at the hotel just outside of Palermo. The view was magnificent, encompassing a pine-clad hillside, interspersed with the brilliance of blossoms below which a shoreline melted into the blue Mediterranean. It was early evening, and a string of lights edged the coastline, while the sound of Sicilian music drifted upward from a club on the waterfront.

It was all so calm and peaceful that she ought to have been relaxed and contented, but instead she listened intently for the drone of aircraft coming in to land or the sound of a car's engine accelerating up the steep road to the hotel.

Getting up, she walked into the room behind her and helped herself to a cigarette. Somehow she had imagined Sir Harold flying to Gitana, obtaining information, and flying straight back, but it was almost thirty-six hours since he had left, and there had been no word from him. Every time the telephone rang when she was in the lounge downstairs she expected the receptionist to call her, but no summons ever came, and her nerves were as taut as violin strings.

Deciding she might as well take a shower before dinner, she went into the bathroom, locking the door behind her and stripping off her clothes. The water here was icy and she moved under the spray vigorously, trying to instil well-being into her body. Then, wrapping herself in a bath-towel, she emerged into the lounge again. She was drying her hair with another towel when there was a sharp knock at the door.

Nicola sighed. What now? She walked resignedly across to open it, keeping herself hidden behind the panels. 'Yes?' she was saying expressionlessly, when her whole being suffused with heat. 'Jason!' she gasped, disbelievingly.

Jason was standing outside looking tall and lean and attractive in a lightweight grey suit, the close-fitting trousers accentuating the muscular strength of his legs. He didn't say anything at once but stood looking at her as she endeavoured, not very successfully, to hide her dishevelled appearance. Then, with deliberate ease, he pushed open the door and entered the room, so that she wrapped her arms around herself to secure the concealing towel.

'Well?' he said at last. 'Aren't you going to say anything?'

Nicola didn't know what to say. She felt hopelessly out of her depth. Jason was much too disturbing a man for her to be entertaining when a bath-towel was her only attire.

'Er – will – will you wait while I put some clothes on?' she whispered uncomfortably.

Jason's dark eyes narrowed. 'What if I say no? What if I say I like you as you are?' he muttered, rather huskily.

Nicola felt as though her legs were turning to water. 'Oh – please,' she murmured unsteadily. 'Just give me a minute.'

Jason lifted his shoulders. 'All right.'

Nicola turned and sped into her bedroom, but once there she didn't wait to dress in case he disappeared again, but wrapped herself in a silk housecoat, and tied the belt securely about her slim waist. Her hair was still damp and hung limply about her shoulders, but there was nothing she could do about that, and make-up would have seemed stupid and artificial after he had seen her without it.

When she emerged, he was standing with his back to her, staring out across the balcony to the coastline beyond. 'Some view,' he said, without turning.

'Yes.' Nicola's voice was still uneven.

'Harold took this suite, I hear.'

'Yes.' There seemed nothing else to add.

Jason turned. 'He seems to treat you very considerately,' he said dryly. 'I wonder why?'

Nicola bent her head. 'He – he asked me to marry him,' she said quietly.

'I know. He told me.' Jason studied her bent head. 'What did you say?'

Nicola looked up. 'Didn't he tell you that, too?'

'No.' Jason's voice was hard. 'You tell me.'

Nicola shivered. 'I – I haven't given him – a – definite answer,' she faltered.

'Oh? Why not? Surely his expectations are sufficient for any woman.'

'Stop being so sarcastic,' she said, looking up rather angrily. 'What – what are you doing here? Wh – where is Sir Harold?'

'In Gitana,' replied Jason, answering her second question first. 'As to the other, I rather thought you wanted to see me.' He stared at her intently. 'To ascertain that I was unharmed!' That was mocking.

Nicola clenched her fists. 'Well, I can see you – you're fine,' she said, unsteadily. 'I'm glad. And – and I'd like to apologize for causing you so much trouble before. Sir – Sir Harold explained what happened.'

'I see.' Jason nodded. He thrust his hands into the pockets of his trousers and came across to her, standing looking down at her with dark disturbing eyes. 'Is that all?'

Nicola's nerves were jumping, and she wished he would move away from her. Close like this all she wanted to do was press herself against him and to hell with the consequences.

'How – how did you get here?' she asked, for something to say.

Jason took one hand out of his pocket and fingered the material of her housecoat. 'By the company jet,' he replied. 'This is nice. Did Sir Harold buy it?'

Nicola's eyes mirrored the hurt he had inflicted. 'You brute!' she said shakily. 'Oh, I wish I'd never come here. I hate you!'

Jason took his other hand out of his pocket and slid it round her, caressing her back very gently. 'Oh, Nicola,' he groaned unsteadily, 'for God's sake, give me some encouragement! Stop behaving like the prim heroine of some nineteenth-century romance. I want you. You know that as well as I do, but do you want me?'

Nicola's face was very close to his. 'Yes,' she said, very softly, 'I want you — you don't know how much!'

Jason pulled her close against him, his mouth seeking the soft scented warmth of her shoulders before finding the parted sweetness of her mouth. His kisses were not gentle, they were hard and passionate and demanding, and Nicola realized that whatever he demanded of her she would give, willingly. Those lean brown hands that she had wanted to touch her aroused her body to the full awareness of her needs, and it was Jason who at last pushed her a little away from him.

'Oh, Nicola,' he muttered thickly, 'I adore you. But unless we stop this now, I won't be able to stop at all!'

His hands were unsteady as he drew out his cigarettes and put one between his lips. When it was lit, he put out a hand and slid it up her bare arm, inside the wide sleeves of the housecoat, as though he couldn't keep his hands off her. Then he pulled her to him again, and said unevenly:

'Harold ought to have had more sense, sending me here alone. You're much too much of a temptation.'

Nicola unbuttoned his jacket and slid her arms round him, pressing her face against his chest. 'I think I'm supposed to be,' she murmured achingly. 'Oh, Jason, I love you, I love you, I love you!'

Jason's arms closed around her, and he muttered: 'Nicola, I ought not to be holding you like this feeling the way I do. Try and understand how self-sacrificing I'm being.' There was a smile in his voice.

Nicola looked up. 'I don't want you to be self-sacrificing,' she whispered daringly.

Jason's eyes darkened. 'Nicola,' he said tautly, 'I'm going to marry you, and I'm prepared to wait a little while longer until I'm legally entitled to make you mine.'

Nicola drew back. 'Are – are you sure you want that? I mean – well, after everything. I was such a pig to you.'

Jason smiled. 'Oh, Nicola, I have no intention of letting Sir Harold Mannering or anyone else have the right to touch you. You're going to be Mrs. Jason Wilde, and I'll do as Harold wants and accept the seat on the board, but first – and most important of all – we're going to have some time away together, even if the pipeline at Castanya never gets completed.'

Nicola's eyes widened. 'Oh, yes, the *coup*!' she exclaimed. 'What's happened?'

Jason drew her down on to the couch at his side. 'Well, it's all over now. Sheikh Mohammed is in exile, I believe, and the Army are in control. I think the trouble he was attempting to cause about me bothering him was the final straw to his ministers. His see-saw game of politics was over.'

'Sir Harold said you attacked him. Did you?'

Jason smiled again. 'Does that appeal to your femi-

186

ninity? That I should fight over you?'

'Not exactly. But it's nice to know you can – if it's necessary,' she replied mischievously.

Jason shook his head. 'Well, anyway, it's all in the past.' His face grew serious. 'Tell me – that day I came to your flat, why didn't you give me a sign – anything – to show you wouldn't have exactly objected to my – well, touching you?' He fingered her hair caressingly.

Nicola sighed. 'I – I thought you couldn't be serious. I mean – after what I'd tried to do to you, I felt sure you must hate me.'

'God!' Jason rested his head back against the soft upholstery. 'If you'd only known! I wanted to strangle you and then when I saw you – I just wanted to love you.'

'I wish you had,' she murmured softly.

'So do I,' he agreed. 'So – now – you'll give Harold his answer, will you? I think he's arriving here late this evening. The jet's gone right back and knowing him he'll be inquisitive enough to want to know the situation.'

Nicola laughed. 'Yes, I'll tell him,' she said. 'By the way, do you think we ought to tell him that I really didn't know you before going out to Castanya?'

Jason leaned over her. 'No. Why should we? That can be our secret. Besides, I feel as though I've known you all my life – or maybe I've just been waiting for you all my life.'

Nicola slid her fingers up his chest. 'Darling, what was that you said about encouragement . . .?'

# Harlequin Presents...

The books that let you escape into the wonderful world of romance! Trips to exotic places...interesting plots...meeting memorable people... the excitement of love....These are integral parts of Harlequin Presents— the heartwarming novels read by women everywhere.

Many early issues are now available. Choose from this great selection!

# Choose from this great selection of exciting Harlequin Presents editions

# Relive a great romance...
# with Harlequin Presents
Complete and mail this coupon today!

## Harlequin Reader Service

In the U.S.A.
1440 South Priest Drive
Tempe, AZ 85281

In Canada
649 Ontario Street
Stratford, Ontario N5A 6W2

Please send me the following Harlequin Presents novels. I am enclosing my check or money order for $1.50 for each novel ordered, plus 75¢ to cover postage and handling.

☐ 99      ☐ 103      ☐ 109
☐ 100      ☐ 106      ☐ 110
☐ 101      ☐ 107      ☐ 111
☐ 102      ☐ 108      ☐ 112

Number of novels checked @ $1.50 each =    $_____

N.Y. and Ariz. residents add appropriate sales tax.    $_____

Postage and handling    $_____.75

TOTAL   $_____

I enclose _____
(Please send check or money order. We cannot be responsible for cash sent through the mail.)

Prices subject to change without notice.

NAME _____
(Please Print)

ADDRESS _____

CITY _____

STATE/PROV. _____

ZIP/POSTAL CODE _____

Offer expires January 31, 1982          107568070